About the Author

After struggling for years to read and trying to hide dyslexia, Bryn Hopkins started to read book after book. If not for his brother handing him that first book, he would not have started writing. Bryn has always had a vivid imagination and now believes that his dyslexia is a positive thing. His first book was released in March of 2022 and gave him a boost of confidence to really believe in himself.

A Broken Heart:
The Black Heart Saga
Book One

Bryn Hopkins

A Broken Heart:
The Black Heart Saga
Book One

Olympia Publishers
London

www.olympiapublishers.com
OLYMPIA PAPERBACK EDITION

Copyright © Bryn Hopkins 2023

The right of Bryn Hopkins to be identified as author of
this work has been asserted in accordance with sections 77 and 78 of
the Copyright, Designs and Patents Act 1988.

All Rights Reserved

No reproduction, copy or transmission of this publication
may be made without written permission.
No paragraph of this publication may be reproduced,
copied or transmitted save with the written permission of the publisher,
or in accordance with the provisions
of the Copyright Act 1956 (as amended).

Any person who commits any unauthorised act in relation to
this publication may be liable to criminal
prosecution and civil claims for damage.

A CIP catalogue record for this title is
available from the British Library.

ISBN: 978-1-80439-249-2

This is a work of fiction.
Names, characters, places and incidents originate from the writer's
imagination. Any resemblance to actual persons, living or dead, is
purely coincidental.

First Published in 2023

Olympia Publishers
Tallis House
2 Tallis Street
London
EC4Y 0AB

Printed in Great Britain

Dedication

I dedicate this book to my late cousin Adam Tomlinson. Born 5 January 1977 and sadly passed away to cancer on 11 June 2019. Adam was an avid reader and lived life to the fullest. He is sadly missed by the entire family.

Acknowledgements

I would love to thank my loving wife Andria who is my constant spell checker. I would like to thank my father James who gets to read my stories first before the go to my publicist and gives me the thumbs up. I would also like to thank my mother; she is probably my biggest fan and gets excited whenever I mention anything about my books. Also, I would like to thank Madison Steel of Saint Pius X school, who won the competition to design the cover for my book.

Prologue

In the beginning, the gods were many and their power was divine. The gods had created all manner of creatures to worship them; goblin, elf, orc and dwarf to name but a few, and through the prayers and admiration of these creatures the gods grew strong.

The gods had given longevity to these races, some more than others, then Ristus had created man, a race of beings that was not long-lived. This new race was violent and wared upon one another. Ristus the god of battle grew strong through the worship of this race called man, and the jealousy of the other gods was great as their power waned. Ristus, now the most powerful of the gods, declared himself ruler of the heavens. In their jealousy, the gods banded together to create a heart-shaped gem, imbuing it with their combined powers so that they could challenge the god of battle, but Sagoth the dark god seized the gem and conquered his siblings. As each of the other gods fell, they released their essence into the world to aid and protect their worshipers.

Sagoth then sought to challenge Ristus, but the god of battles' strength was far greater than that of the dark god and he defeated Sagoth, wounding him gravely. Ristus banished Sagoth and stripped him of his powers and cast him from the heavens. The gem had become corrupted by the death and blood of the sleighed gods, turning as black as the soul of Sagoth himself. The dark god clung to life by use of the gem's power, waiting for the day his strength would return, then would he challenge Ristus once more.

The orcs had built a great fortress in the black mountain ranges to honour their fallen god. Sagoth had dwelt within the fortress for five millennia, all the while his followers' offering prayers and worship. The dark god of the orcs had finally been reborn, calling himself the demon lord of hell and ordered his legions to go forth and conquer this world of men, thus the demon grew stronger with every man slain, his powers slowly growing. But the world of man was not so easily beaten. These savage beings banded together with other races of this world to stop the orcs and their lord and his quest for power.

Chapter One

Orcs, trolls and goblins fled the field of battle as the armies of man, dwarf and elf had united to stand against the demon lord Sagoth, his quest for blood and power had forged the unity between the races. Sagoth, beaten and wounded, had retreated back to his stronghold, the Dark Fortress. Now the fortress was ablaze and surrounded on all sides, besieged by armies.

Sagoth dropped to one knee. The blow from the dwarven war hammer had split his black steel armour, snapping at least three ribs.

Dunan iron fist stood before the demon lord. "Do you yield, you black-hearted son of a goat?"

Sagoth's hand flashed up towards Dunan's throat. A white shafted arrow slammed through Sagoth's palm, followed by another that slammed into his shoulder, causing his attack to falter. Alinar, the crowned king of the elves, aimed another arrow at the demon.

"The dwarf asked if you yielded," said Alinar, his gold and white armour reflecting the fire light.

Sagoth reached up and pulled his black-horned helm from his head. Oval violet eyes stared with malevolence at the two foes in front of him.

"And if I yield?" asked the demon lord.

"Then you will be imprisoned never to see the light of day again," said Alinar.

Sagoth laughed and rose to his feet. His black armour glinted a deep crimson red in the fire light. The demon lord stood at seven feet tall, his pale white skin shone with perspiration, his long grey hair hung limp and sweat-drenched.

"Foolish creatures, I hold the power of the Black Heart Gem. Even if you succeed in striking me down, I will not die; I will dwell in the bowels of hell till I'm summoned again." His left hand reached up and lovingly stroked a fist-sized gem embedded in the chest plate of his armour.

"Then die and return to hell," came a voice from behind. King Tyrin Degarre ran forward, plunging his sword through the demon's back. The blade burst through Sagoth's chest, dislodging the black gem. Sagoth screamed out as Tyrin pulled his blade free.

"Do not let him touch you," warned Elazar.

The mage was uttering an incantation, but the demon lord spun and seized Tyrin by his silver breast plate and throat.

"You shall provide me with the sacrifice needed for my return, I curse you and your bloodline. From your kin, a child shall be born with a mark upon him, and when the three moons align, he will be sacrificed and the gateways of hell shall open. This I seal with blood." Sagoth pulled a black-bladed dagger from his belt and drew it across his own throat. Black blood sprayed forth, covering Tyrin's face and drenching his silver armour.

Elazar finished the incantation. White chains of fire sprang from the ground and lashed to the wrists of the demon lord, dragging him to his knees. Dunan ran forward, striking Sagoth in the chest knocking him to his back.

Elazar spoke the words of power and flames blazed around Sagoth, engulfing him; the flames burnt so bright that it forced all of them to turn away. Finally, the flames subsided. There was no sign of Sagoth; the demon lord had gone, only the black gem remained.

Dunan ran to Tyrin's side. "Are you OK, my friend?" he asked.

Tyrin wretched once more. "Bring me water, elf," shouted Dunan.

"You have the manners of an orc," replied Alinar, handing his water pouch to Tyrin who accepted it gratefully.

"What did Sagoth say to you?" asked Elazar.

Tyrin took another drink and swilled the blood from his mouth. He repeated to the others what Sagoth had said.

When he'd finished, Elazar was the first to speak. "The alignment is not for another hundred years. I will take the gem back to High Castle and with the help of my fellow mages we may be able to find a way to stop the curse."

"I can stop the curse," said Dunan, hefting his hammer. "I'll smash that damn thing right now."

"That would be pointless," put in Elazar. "You could smash it into a thousand pieces and those pieces would find a way to join back together, it is said to contain the essences of all the fallen gods."

"Then let me take it back to the Grey Mountains, I will bury it so deep that no one will ever find it."

"I hate to agree with the dwarf," put in Alinar, "but if we divided the power of the gem, we increase our chances of stopping the curse."

Tyrin stood. "I must agree with Dunan and Alinar," he said.

"So, it's settled," said Dunan, raising his hammer.

"Stay your hand, Master Dwarf," bellowed Elazar. "If you strike that gem without my help, you will kill us all."

Dunan froze. Elazar smoothed down his blue robes.

"Show me your hammer."

Dunan held out the twenty-pound war hammer with one hand, its dark grey steel head had runes engraved in the metal, the three-foot wooded shaft was made from black ebony and wrapped with leather. Elazar placed his hands on either side of the hammer head and started to whisper an incantation. Slowly, the hammer started to glow. The steel becoming brighter and brighter until it shone as bright as polished silver.

"Be ready," said Elazar. "Strike the gem when I say."

The mage stood back, closed his eyes, raised his arms and started to whisper.

The others watched as two orbs of light formed on the palms of his hands. The orbs shifted in colour from white to yellow then orange and red. Finally, the red turned to purple then to black.

"Now!" shouted Elazar, releasing the two orbs. Dunan swung the hammer with all his might, striking the gem at the same time as the orbs.

Darkness engulfed the four companions – so black that none could see their hand in front of their face. Slowly, the darkness withdrew as Elazar cast a second spell. The Black Heart Gem of Sagoth lay on the floor now broken into four pieces, all as clear as crystal.

Elazar spoke, "Each of you must take a piece. Do not hold to it for it will seek to corrupt you and make itself whole again. Bind the gem in gold; it will dampen its power. Tell no one of the gems, you are now its guardians."

"Where has the darkness gone?" asked Alinar.

"It has not gone," replied Elazar. "It is out in our world seeking a new host."

Dunan thrust out his now silver hammer. "I swear by my blood and my hammer, no one shall have the piece protected by the dwarves."

Tyrin laid his sword to the hammer. "I swear by my blood and on my sword, none shall take the piece guarded by man."

Finally, Alinar crossed the weapons with his bow. "I, too, swear by my blood that the elves shall guard this piece."

Elazar gathered one of the pieces, tucked it inside his blue robe then spoke a word of power and vanished. The air around the others crackled with energy. Tyrin turned to Dunan and offered his hand. Dunan took his hand in the warrior's grip.

"Thank you, my friend," said Tyrin.

"Think nothing of it," replied Dunan. "Should you need me and my lads again, just send out the call to arms." Dunan turned towards Alinar. "Elf," he said as he waked past and collected the gem piece.

Tyrin smiled at the lack of friendliness between the other two leaders.

"Why do the dwarves and elves hate each other?" Tyrin asked.

"It's not that we hate them, the dwarves are jealous of our longevity," replied Alinar. "You and Dunan will not be here for the alignment, I will be should the Gods permit it, and I will lead my armies to stop his return once more."

Tyrin thrust out his hand to the elf king. "There should be trade between our peoples, it would be good for all if there were."

"We shall see," said Alinar, taking the hand and smiling. The elf king turned, gathered a piece of the gem and walked away.

Tyrin looked at the blade of his sword; the black blood of Sagoth still lay upon the steel. Using the sleeve of his jerking, Tyrin wiped the blade, but the steel did not wipe clean, the blood of the demon lord had absorbed into the very steel, looking as if black rivers of blood ran down the length of the blade.

Chapter Two

Elazar opened his eyes. He was back in the courtyard of High Castle. The sun was just starting to rise, bathing the castle in a warm orange glow. The castle sat atop High Mountain. At this altitude, the weather should have been freezing, but the spell that protected the inhabitants also kept the climate comfortable. The castle had been built by the mages of this world for those gifted by magic. It boasted over one hundred rooms and an extensive library, but most impressive was the grand hall where the four masters would hold council and teach potential new mages.

The four towers of High Castle all faced towards each major compass point. Ebras the last grand master had explained to Elazar that the position of the towers drew the power from the land, enhancing the spell that protected the castle.

A student in green robes came from one of the livestock building. Seeing the blue robes of a master, she placed her basket of eggs on the floor and hurried over. "Can I be of assistance, Master?" she asked. All the inhabitants of High Castle were expected to help out and earn their keep.

Elazar looked at the student and couldn't remember her name. "Do you know if the coals have been lit in the bath house?" asked Elazar.

"No, Master, the bath house is still cold. Would you like me to prepare it for you?"

"No, thank you," he replied, "I will see to it myself."

The student bowed once more and hurried away to continue

with her duties.

Elazar entered the bath house. The room was cold and dark. Uttering a word of power, the torches and candles instantly ignited, casting a warm glow around the room. Elazar caught his reflection in one of the bronze mirrors. His blue robes were filthy and stank of smoke, his normally oiled black hair and beard looked unkempt and messy.

Ten bronze bathtubs stood with fresh water in them. The floor of the bath house had been laid with white marble tiles that reflected the light from the torches. On the far wall was a mosaic map that depicted the land of Sharr. Elazar had always admired the mosaic map. In its centre stood High Castle Mountain, surrounded by the Savage Steppes, a desert which stretched for hundreds of miles in all directions. the Steppes was a harsh and perilous place and was the home to the Chimbai tribes, a nomadic people.

To the east stood the capital city of Carthage, home of the Degarre dynasty. The king had built his palace on the island. Centuries ago, great earthquakes had caused the eastern mountains to topple, closing off the narrow inlet which had let the sea inland. Tyrin's ancestor the first king of Sharr had chosen the island for its defensive position. Surrounded on all sides now by the trapped sea. The island was the ultimate fortress.

With the palace in the centre of the island, the city of Carthage had grown around it. Tyrin's rule extended across the land that had been divided up into duchies and baronies under the rule of minor nobles, all of which fought for power but ultimately answered to the king.

From Carthage, one could travel south through the duchy of Yada across the Jade River and on to the vast grass planes of Varith, which stretched for hundreds of miles. Farm settlements were dotted all over the planes and life was hard for the farmers working those lands, raising cattle for slaughter.

The planes of Varith extended all the way south until it reached the Great Forest of the elves. Not much was known of the elves; the most common knowledge about them was their skill with a bow. Humans were not permitted into their lands. Elazar had once visited the Great Forest only on the invite of King Alinar. The mage had always thought High Castle was a wonderment to behold, but it paled in significance to the home of the elves.

The elves had used the trees themselves as their homes, the trees had not been felled. Instead, it seemed that the giant trees had been hollowed out, creating passageways from one tree to another; the branches interlocking with one another, creating paths and walkways. Elazar watched as the elves passed from tree to tree, his vision had blurred as he tried to focus on the tree tops, much to the amusement of King Alinar. Beyond the elven borders, to the south lay a desolate wasteland. The only creatures rumoured to live there were the ogres, docile and rarely seen. Every now and then, an ogre would wander into the realm of the elves looking for food.

Casting his eyes to the west, to where the Great Forest ended and the marsh lands started, these extended to the fishing islands and villages and the ports of Ventcana. Continuing west, one would finally come to the Grey Mountains, home of the dwarves and the valleys beyond which ended at the western sea.

Lastly, Elazar looked to the north. Only a few settlements of men were this high up, away from the protection of the king's armies. The northern most village was Hollowrock, situated twenty miles away from the borders of Dark Wood. The woods had been named for the black wooded tree that grew there; the foliage of the trees was a dark green that from a distance looked as black as the tree trunks themselves. Beyond the Dark Wood stood the Black Mountain range, a vast wilderness home to the orcs and their clans which were scattered throughout the mountains, and in its centre stood the Dark Fortress of Sagoth.

Beyond the mountains not much was known of the land. If someone were to make it through the mountains, past the orcs, then they would come to the swamps of Noras; home of the goblins and all manner of other creatures, and beyond that the frozen tundra, home of the great white bears.

Now had come the discovery of a new continent far to the south east. One of the king's fishing vessels had been caught in a storm on the Eastern Sea and had been considered lost. A year or so later, the ship had returned laden with gold and silver, the captain and the surviving crew had told of a vast tropical continent where a colony of dark-skinned dwarves had taken them in and cared for them.

Tyrin had sent a ship to the new land. He had asked Elazar to send a representative from High Castle to open trade between the two realms. Elazar had sent Lady Shamari. She had been gone now for over a year. Elazar had received reports from Shamari that had been sent by way of magic – these reports had been sent to Tyrin and his council – trade between the two nations would be difficult due to the distance. Shamari and Elazar could commune through the use of their powers, but now Tyrin had tasked the mages of High Castle to come up with a way for the two nations to be able to trade without the need for the long voyage.

"What you ask of me, Tyrin, would take tremendous amounts of power," said Elazar. "I am able to teleport myself over great distances, but I'm not sure I could travel that far never mind transport cargo."

It was Lady Shamari that had come up with the idea of constructing a magical gateway on both continents which would allow safe passage, eliminating the need for the long voyage.

"What you are proposing would take great amounts of magical energy," said Elazar. "You will be on the other side of the world on your own. The work could take you years to accomplish."

"It is a job I am willing to undertake," she had replied.

Work had started on the gateway almost immediately in Carthage, some of the most powerful students had been sent to build the focal point, while Lady Shamari would build the one in Rainoa.

Elazar turned his attention back to the baths; waving a hand across one of the tubs and uttering a word of power, steam started to rise from the water. Removing his dirty clothes, the mage stepped into the bath and sighed with pleasure; the warm water felt good against his skin. The battle with Sagoth had drained him more than he thought. Elazar leaned back in the bath and closed his eyes.

Elazar was sat in the great hall. The young mage Kadius had completed his training and had been given the rank of master. The dark-haired twenty-year-old had been delighted and stood resplendent in his blue robes when a student burst into the hall and bowed.

"Excuse me, Masters, but there is a dwarf at the gates asking to speak with you. He says that if we don't open the gate, he will smash it open."

Elazar chuckled. "Please show our guest in."

A few minutes later, Dunan, High Chief of the dwarves,

strode into the hall followed by a young dwarf.

"To what do we owe the pleasure of your company, Master Dwarf?" asked Elazar.

"Stop trying to flatter me, you dressed up trickster," snapped Dunan. "I need you to take in this lad."

"Why?" interrupted Kadius. "And a more pressing matter; how did you manage to get to our gates uninvited?"

Dunan scoffed. "You live on a mountain. I'm a dwarf. The journey here is but a pleasant walk for us. Now will you take in the boy?"

"And why should we take in a dwarf child?" asked Elazar.

The youngster stood stock still, his head bowed, looking at the floor.

"Well," snapped Dunan, "show them what you can do."

The youngster stepped forward and snapped his fingers together. Instantly, a ball of flames leapt from his hand and landed on the floor, setting the blue carpet alight.

Elazar waved his hand and instantly the fire disappeared, leaving no mark upon the carpet.

"So, will you take the lad?" asked Dunan. "He nearly burnt down the bakery and two grain stores."

"Remarkable," said Elazar. "Do you know what this means?"

"Yes," answered Dunan, "I would have to rebuild the bakery and the grain stores if this lad can't learn to control his gift."

"No," said Elazar, "you irritating dwarf, he is the first of his kind to display magical talent. This is amazing!"

"So, you'll have him?" asked Dunan.

"Of course, we will," put in Kadius.

A noise woke Elazar; one of the students had come to prepare the bathhouse. The student was a small blue-scaled creature that had a shock of red hair running down the centre of its head which continued down its spine. It had large pupil-less eyes and its teeth were like rows of needles. When it spoke, its words were more of a hiss than actual words.

"Excuse me, Master, I did not mean to wake you."

"That's all right," said Elazar. "I hadn't realised I had fallen asleep."

"May I be of assistance, Master?" asked the creature.

"Please pass me a towel," answered the mage.

The small creature opened a wooden cupboard containing fresh white towels and handed one to the mage.

"Thank you," said Elazar. "You're a Gablukk, aren't you?" asked Elazar.

"Yes," replied the creature. "My name is Yaslin."

"Tell me, Yaslin, are you happy here?"

"Why yes, Master, my people are so few now it is nice to feel and be safe here. The goblins and orcs have hunted my kind for generations. We are a peaceful people and refuse to fight."

"How have you survived all these years being hunted?" asked Elazar.

The little creature's mouth opened, showing its needle-like teeth. Elazar took this to be a smile.

"My people have the ability to merge through rock and stone and we can change the colour of our scales to blend in with our surroundings."

"Why do the orcs hunt you?" asked Elazar.

"We are considered a delicacy," replied Yaslin.

"Oh," said Elazar, trying to hide the shock from his face.

"There are less than a hundred of us left now," said Yaslin, "but my people have found solace living in the mountain below.

The nomads of the desert leave us in peace; they are a hardy but peaceful people. Will there be anything else, Master?"

"No, thank you," replied Elazar. "I must see the other masters and tell them what has happened."

Yaslin bowed and carried on preparing the bathhouse for the students.

For thirty years now, more and more people and creatures of all manner had started displaying magical abilities, and a new age of magic had begun.

Chapter Three

The steel grey stallion stumbled for the third time. Tyrin reined him in, dismounted and stroked the horse's neck. He spoke softly to it. The stallion nuzzled its head into Tyrin's shoulder, then sneezed, which made Tyrin laugh.

"Well, Shadow my friend, we have been travelling for over a month and we have both smelt and looked better," he said, looking down at his travel-stained black clothes.

"Your Majesty," came the voice of General Kaylin as he approached on his chestnut mare. He reined in his horse and dismounted. "I think we should camp here for the night; both men and horses are tired and if we continue, some of our wounded won't make it back to the capital."

Tyrin eyed the general and noticed he looked tired; bags were under his keen grey eyes and he had forgone his daily shave and now sported a black beard flecked with silver that matched his hair. At fifty-five years old, Kaylin was the most trusted man in Tyrin's army. He had been the king's champion for twenty years and his skills with a blade were deadly.

Tyrin smiled at the general. "You are right, my friend. Have the officers make preparations for the army to rest for two days, but find me ten men who can still ride and enough horses for each man to have two spare mounts. I will continue on to Carthage. We are less than two days away and I want to get back and inform the councillors of what has happened."

"It will be as you say, Your Majesty, but it will be nine men.

I shall accompany you."

"No," Tyrin replied, "you will remain with the army and see that every man here makes it home."

"Now look here, lad," said Kaylin, forgetting all formalities. "I'm your champion and my place is by your side, I can still best any man here with a blade, including a young pup like you."

Tyrin's laughter boomed out. "General Kaylin, if I didn't know any better, I'd say that you were disobeying an order."

"A pox on your orders; I may be getting older, but I'm still unbeaten in any tourney."

Tyrin walked to the general and placed his hand on his shoulder. "The army needs its general, not its king. Bring our men home to the hero's welcome they deserve. I will be fine without you this one time."

Kaylin relaxed. "It will be as you say, lad," he said with a smile. "I will select the men myself," he said as he swung onto the saddle.

Kaylin loved the young king; he was wise beyond his thirty years. Even dressed as he was in his travel-stained clothes of black woollen leggings and leather jerkin, the blond-haired, blue-eyed monarch still looked regal. He was wide of shoulder and narrow of hip and his boyish face was handsome. Kaylin rode back towards the army and called a halt. None of the soldiers wore any armour, all wore simple wool leggings and woollen shirts; the silver armour of the soldiers had been stored in the wagons, making the ride home more comfortable. Of the three armies that had gone to the Black Mountains, Tyrin's had suffered the greatest loss. Fifteen thousand fighting men had left and now only nine thousand three hundred and forty-two were returning, with four hundred and eleven injured. Regiments of soldiers had departed back to their dutchies as they passed through.

Tyrin could hear General Kaylin shouting out his orders and watched with pride as the officers and men started to set up camp. He felt a push on his back, the stallion nudged him once more. Tyrin turned and stroked the horse's nose.

"No, Shadow," he said, "you will stay here and rest, you're tired and could hurt us both if I rode you."

The stallion started to stamp its front hoof on the ground as if in protest. "Now, now," said Tyrin. "Is that any way for the king's horse to behave?" The horse continued to stamp its hoof. "If you behave, I'll see that Kaylin feeds you extra carrots." Shadow stopped and his ears pricked up. "I thought as much," chuckled Tyrin.

An hour later, with the cook fires lit and the army settled in, Tyrin and his ten men thundered out of the camp, leading their spare mounts.

Tyrin and his men had pushed the horses hard. Three of the horses had died from exhaustion and now the men were down to their last mounts, they had entered the duchy of Movale, the second largest city in the land of Sharr.

The hooves of the horses sounded like thunder on the cobbles as they rode through the streets in the early morning hours. The city patrol had rushed out, blocking the main street which led through the city, and stopped the eleven riders. The captain had eyed the mounted men suspiciously; all were wearing black wool leggings and leather riding cloaks with black knee-high riding boots, and all were travel-stained with dust.

"What in the hell is going on?" asked the captain of the watch; a tall pocked-faced man.

Corporal Derrel Mendez nudged his horse forward. "Stand

aside, man, we're in a hurry," he demanded.

"On whose authority are you riding through the duke's city at this ungodly hour?"

Corporal Mendez was growing more irritated by the second. "We are the king's men and need to get back to Carthage. Now stand aside."

The captain heeled his horse forward to block their path even more. "If you are king's men and on the king's business, where are your papers?"

Mendez drew his sword and smashed the pommel into the captain's face, causing him to topple from his saddle.

The men of the watch were about to draw their weapons when Tyrin pushed his horse forward and pulled his hood back and showed the gold signet ring on his right hand, bearing the royal seal of two crossed swords encircled by a crown.

"Will this suffice?" asked Tyrin, his voice was cold and unfriendly.

The men of the watch snapped to attention as they recognised the king.

"Please forgive us, Your Majesty, we are only following orders," said one of the men, stepping aside to allow Tyrin and his men to continue.

Corporal Mendez was the last to leave; he turned to the men of the watch.

"I would take him to see a healer," said the corporal, pointing to the unconscious captain. "I heard his nose break, and he struck his head as he landed. When he wakes, tell him Corporal Derrel Mendez was the one who struck him, if he wishes another lesson in manners." Derrel heeled his horse into a run and followed after the king.

It was midday when Tyrin and his men disembarked from the ferry. The white walls of the city were a welcome site. Fresh horses were waiting for the king and his men; it would still take them around an hour and a half of hard riding to reach the palace grounds. The eleven horses were lathered in sweat as the riders cantered through the streets of Carthage. They turned onto the busy avenue of the market area where the streets were packed with the citizens going about their daily business. The lead soldiers were shouting at the townsfolk to step aside; angry shouts and jeers were hurled back at the riders as they galloped past. One trader picked an orange from his stall and threw it at the riders. It sailed past the head of Corporal Mendez and hit Tyrin on his back. Derrel dragged on his reins; his horse came skidding to a stop. Dismounting, Derrel Mendez turned to see a chubby balding man who stood open-mouthed, holding another orange in his hand. Quickly, the chubby man placed the orange back on the stall.

"Name," demanded Derrel, walking over and jabbing his finger into the chubby trader's chest.

"Jones, sir, Arron Jones," replied the man.

"Well, Arron Jones, report to the soldiers' barracks at the palace at sunset. Ask for Corporal Mendez and don't be late."

"Yes, sir," said the chubby trader.

Derrel turned, mounted his horse and galloped away. Derrel Mendez approached the main gates of the palace and the two sentries saluted as he trotted through. The gelding was tired; its head hanging low. As he entered the stabbing area, he saw the nine men who had accompanied him were stood talking; they had all been chosen by General Kaylin to accompany the king back to his city and now they stood awaiting their next orders. Derrel Mendez was not much older than the nine men who had rode with him, but he had rose to the rank of corporal quickly. At twenty years old, Derrel Mendez had shown the natural leaderships skills needed to progress his career in the army. Most of the senior officers had said it was because of his father, General Kaylin Mendez, that his son Derrel had been promoted; this had led to Derrel challenging anyone and everyone to a duel. The rumours had soon stopped when Derrel had won his first five duel easily, the fifth dual had seen a sergeant nearly dead; it was only Derrel's skill with the blade that had saved the sergeant from being skewered through the heart. Now the only rumour he heard was, could Derrel beat his father in a dual? This always made him laugh. One of the soldiers saw him approaching and saluted which caused the others to snap to attention. A stable boy ran forward as the corporal dismounted.

"Brush him down with hay, boy, don't let the sweat dry on him. Give him water and then place a feed bag on him."

"Yes, sir," said the boy, leading the horse away.

Derrel saluted back to the waiting men. "Stand easy, men," said Derrel. The soldiers relaxed.

"Orders, sir?" asked a young blond-haired man.

Derrel pulled a leather pouch from his belt and produced nine silver pieces. "Go to the western quarter, there you will find a tavern called the Bow and Quiver. There is a whore house next to it; tell the lady of the house that Corporal Mendez has sent you. She will give you all a bed for the night and a woman to keep you warm." He placed the nine silvers into the blond-haired soldier's hand. The men smiled, thanked the corporal and set off to take their pleasures.

Corporal Mendez entered the officers' quarters. A young dark-haired squire came running to his side and noted the travel-stained clothes. The corporal always took pride in his appearance; his long black hair was always oiled, his uniform spotless and his handsome face never had the stubble on it that was there now. The squire looked the corporal up and down and raised an eyebrow.

"Well, you look like shit," said the squire.

Derrel smiled. "Go prepare me a bath and get me a clean set of clothes." The squire turned to leave. "Tal," said Derrel, calling after the boy, "you do know that if you talk to the other officers like that, they will give you demerits and you could find yourself in the stocks."

The youth smiled. "I know, but you're my older brother and I like being a pain to you."

Derrel threw his boot at his brother; the youth dodged out of the way and ran off laughing. At thirteen years old, Tal had the reflexes of a cat; unlike Derrel, he lacked the discipline of his older brother. Their father had assigned Tal as Derrel's squire in hopes that some of his older brother's discipline would rub off on the youngster.

Derrel Mendez stood looking at his reflection in the polished bronze mirror. His hair was neatly oiled, his clothes clean and fresh, Tal had polished his black riding boots to a high shine. The grey woollen trousers and shirt were made of the softest wool and felt good against his skin. Corporal Mendez made his way towards the soldiers' barracks. The sun was setting in the west, turning the sky to a ruddy orange. The night was warm as Derrel rounded the corner; he could hear the raised voice of a woman. Two guards were stood being yelled at by the most beautiful woman Derrel had ever seen. The blonde-haired woman was around five-and-a-half-feet tall. Her hair was the colour of golden straw and her eyes were sapphire blue. She wore a simple dress of blue cotton and behind her stood the little fat trader Arron

Jones, clutching a large fruit basket to his chest.

"What the hell is going on here?" demanded Derrel.

The young woman fixed her blue eyes on the corporal and a chill ran through his body; the stare was icy, and her face was flushed with anger.

"You," said the woman, stepping into the corporal's path, "you're the one who nearly trampled my father with your horse and then had the nerve to order him to come and report to you—"

"Your father," interrupted Derrel, "struck the king; a crime punishable by death. Your father should be hanging from the gallows in the town square." The little trader paled and tried to speak, but his daughter cut him off.

"I'm sure the king is quite all right the orange was ripe and soft, so I assume that there is not a mark on his royal body."

Derrel was about to reply when a deep commanding voice broke through the arguing.

"The king is fine and he would also like to know what all this noise is about."

Derrel and the guards snapped to attention as King Tyrin walked into sight. He was now wearing soft leather leggings and tunic that had been dyed to a deep blue. The blonde woman and her father bowed as the monarch approached.

"Your Majesty," began Derrel, "as we entered the market today, this man threw an orange that struck you. I asked him to report here to receive his punishment."

"Forgive my rudeness, Your Majesty," said the young woman, bowing low, "but my father had no idea that it was you he struck; he simply acted out of anger at nearly being trampled on by you and your men."

Tyrin looked at the trader, who stood wide-eyed and dumbly nodded his head. "My father wishes to offer his most profound apologies and hopes His Majesty will accept this gift from him." Arron thrust out the basket of fruit.

Tyrin smiled. "Firstly, young lady, I would ask your name."

"Emelia," replied the woman.

"Second, Emelia, it is I who should offer your father an apology for my behaviour earlier; the corporal here was only doing his duty in protecting me." Tyrin turned to Arron and bowed his head. "Please forgive me, Master Trader, and I will accept the gift and by way of a thanks, I would like your daughter to return here tomorrow night and join me for dinner."

"She will, Your Majesty," said the little man gaining some confidence.

"Excellent," said Tyrin, taking Emelia by the hand and kissing it. "My carriage will take you home and will collect you tomorrow, I look forward to seeing you. Corporal, please see to the arrangements and then join me in my private quarters."

Derrel saluted as the king turned and walked away.

Chapter Four

Dunan, High Chief of the Dwarves, came to a halt. At sixty years old, the dwarf leader didn't look his age. His coal dark beard and hair only had a few specks of silver in it. His men had been marching now for three weeks and even Dunan's prodigious strength was starting to wane. All dwarves were known for their strength and stamina; a dwarven warrior was three times stronger than any human and could run for a day and a night and still have the strength to swing the heavy hammers or axes they used in battle.

Of the five thousand dwarves that had joined the battle, three thousand eight hundred and fifty-six were returning home. Dunan watch with pride as his men still marched in formation. Most had removed the battle helms of polished iron and looped them to their belts. The brown buck skin boots and trousers were covered in dust as well as the black fur jerkins they wore over the chainmail undercoats. The army was now less than three miles from the entrance to the Grey Mountain pass. The pass would be guarded on both sides, the thick oak and elm forest provided great cover for the dwarf sentries who stood guard. The forest backed on to the Grey cliffs, which dropped for over several hundred feet, making the pass the only access to the valleys and the mountains beyond which were home to the dwarves.

The pass only measured thirty feet in width but stretched on for over a mile. The dwarves had removed hundreds of tonnes of rock, making the cliff face smooth and removing any hand holds, making it impossible to climb. The pass was death for any army that tried to go through. Huge boulders had been positioned on the clifftops that could be dropped on an advancing army, causing mass carnage. The low dulcet sound of the dwarven war horn sounded, one of the marching dwarves lifted a horn to his lips and sent out an answering reply. Ten dwarfs came running from the tree line to greet the returning army. A young dwarf with copper red hair and a short beard raised his hammer in salute.

"Hail Dunan, High chief of the Grey Mountains."

Dunan rolled his eyes at the use of his title. "Well met, Lubik," answered Dunan.

"You look tired, My Lord. Are you well?"

"I'd be better if you'd drop the formalities and stopped kissing my arse," replied Dunan. The other dwarves in earshot started to laugh as the youngster reddened. "Be a good lad and run on ahead and tell them to prepare a feast for our lads; we're all ready for a good meal and we all need a well-deserved drink. Tell my wife to break out the good mead."

Lubik bowed then set off at a run. As the last of the dwarves came through the pass, the sun was starting to set, bathing the mountains in an orange glow. The valley containing the homes of the dwarves was a hive of activity as wives and children ran out to meet returning husbands and fathers. Every house built in the valley had been constructed from the mined rocks and stone of the mountains, even the roofs were made from stone. The building prowess of the dwarves was known throughout the land of Sharr.

As the stone was mined, the dwarves had mastered the ability to split and cut the hard grey granite into six-by-twelve-inch pieces, creating roof tiles. Each one was expertly cut to lock to the next tile. All the homes had been set out in rows, giving each dwarf the same amount of land as the next. Not one family owned more than the next; this brought a sense of peace amongst the dwarves. In the very centre stood the hall of the high lord, a two-storey building where the elders would meet and hold council. Dunan heard his name called and saw his wife running towards him, her long brown hair was now streaked with silver that hung in braids from her temples. She flew into her husband's out-stretched arms and kissed his bearded cheek. Her tears flowed freely.

"Hush now, woman, I told you I'd come home to you."

"That you did," said Varela, wiping her tears on the sleeves of her green dress.

"Where are the boys?" Dunan asked.

Varela smiled. "In the mine, as usual; they have been working nonstop ever since you left. Nerath and his workers broke through into a new chamber last week and reported a chasm that no one has been able to reach the bottom of. Nerath dropped a rock off the edge and never heard it hit the bottom. Skamet tells me we will have to bridge the chasm to reach the other side. He is designing the bridge himself."

Dunan smiled at the mention of his sons' names. Grabbing hold of a passing youth, Dunan relayed orders to go and fetch his two sons.

That night, the valley of the dwarves was filled with music and laughter. Early the next morning, Dunan woke his sons. The three of them sat down to a breakfast of bread cheese and cold ham. Dunan felt a sense of pride looking at his sons; both of them had long braided brown hair and beards. Nerath was three years older than his brother, Skamet, yet they looked like twins.

"I need you to show me this chasm you've found, but first I want to call past Gyon's. I need him to make something for me."

"The jewellers?" asked Nerath. "He was quite drunk last night, Father. I don't think he'll be awake yet."

"Well, he will be soon," said Dunan with a smile.

"This must be a very important piece of jewellery for Mother," said Skamet, smiling.

Dunan looked at his sons. "What I'm about to tell you is important and must not be repeated." He placed a small leather pouch on the table. He untied the leather throngs and tipped out a small gem.

"Pretty," said Nerath, "but I don't think that Mother would like it."

Skamet reached for the gem.

"Do not touch it," snapped his father. Skamet froze. "I need to tell you where that came from and what must be done." Dunan told his sons of the battle with Sagoth and of the splitting of the gem, and of the curse the demon had placed upon Tyrin.

Nerath was the first to speak. "You plan to encase the gem and drop it into the chasm."

Dunan nodded his head. "I also want to drop tonnes of rock down there with it; all rock that we take from the mines will be brought to the chasm and we will try and fill it."

"That will bring suspicion from the workers," put in Skamet.

"I'll deal with the workers," said Dunan, "now finish your breakfast and let's go wake Gyon."

Chapter Five

All had been chaos on the battlefield; the goblins had been the first to break and run. The trolls had seen the goblins take flight and followed after them, this had left the right flank of the orc army open to Dunan and his dwarves; they had hit the right flank, smashing their way through. Panic had set in and the remaining orc army had fled.

The scream and cries of the orcs echoed through the cave systems that ran through the Black Mountains. A few of the larger clans had gathered in a vast cave and fights had broken out amongst the orcs. The few goblins that had remained were turned upon; their deaths were quick and brutal, limbs were torn from bodies. Some were impaled on the stalagmites within the cave. The fighting ceased when Urag, leader of the Bear Skull clan, blew on his war horn.

"Why are we fighting amongst ourselves? The enemy is back there, we outnumbered the enemy and still we fled the battle."

"It was the goblins; they fled, leaving us open to an attack," said an orc, bleeding from a wound across his chest.

Urag raised his spiked mace. "No more will orcs kill orcs. We need to be as one clan and fight our enemies."

The surrounding orcs shifted nervously, the tension in the cave was at breaking point; one wrong move and the fighting would start again.

A stocky warrior pushed his way to the front. "And who will

lead this one clan? You?"

"I am Margrel, leader of the Grey Wolves, and I would rather drink goblin piss than take orders from a Bear Skull."

Margrel's face disappeared as Urag swung his mace, smashing in the head of the Grey Wolves' leader. Black blood sprayed over the nearest orcs. Before anyone could react, Urag's voice thundered out around the cave.

"If orcs must fight orcs, let the clan leaders step forth and it will be us who fight. I claim the Grey Wolves as mine; I have killed their chief. Will anyone challenge me?"

No one moved; the Bear Skull tribe was one of the largest of the clans and Urag was well-known for his fighting skills. Urag was still young when he had challenged his father for the right to lead the Bear Skull clan. The fight had been over quickly. Urag was big for an orc; he stood at over six feet tall and was powerfully built.

Xegthanuuth had led the Bear Skull tribe for over twenty years. All the other clan leaders had heard how Urag had toyed with his father in the battle, wounding him in several places before delivering the death blow. Now Urag stood covered in the blood of humans, dwarves and elves, openly challenging the other leaders.

A tall warrior pushed his way to the front and stood before Urag. He was dressed in a white bear skin, the head of the bear sat atop his head. "I am Xruul of the White Bears. If my clan follows you, what do you offer?"

Urag stepped forward and placed a hand on Xruul's shoulder. "If you follow me, I promise that we will kill all our enemies. We will wipe the humans from the land, take their cities and destroy them. We will build the largest army the humans have ever seen."

Xruul drew his dagger and sliced open the palm of his hand. He placed it on Urag's chest. "The White Bears are yours to command."

Another orc stepped forward. "I am Vorgak, I command the Long Spears. I too wish to destroy the humans." Vorgak repeated the blood oath.

One by one, the leaders of the clans stepped forward. The Lizard Claw, followed by the Axe Heads and the Green Snakes all swore the oath. Finally, a small orc limped forward. He was blind in one eye that had a jagged scar running through it.

The orc bowed. "I am Mug of the Raven Claw. My clan was nearly wiped out by the dwarves. If you will have me, I will join."

"Swear the oath," said Urag, handing a dagger to Mug. The little orc drew the blade across his hand and placed it to Urag's chest.

Alinar stood at the front of the returning army. The elves had been marching for weeks now. The journey had taken longer for the elves for they had avoided the towns and villages of men. The land had provided food and water for the marching elven army. Alinar had led three thousand of the finest archers in Sharr from the Great Forest to aid King Tyrin. It was well known to all that elven warriors were deadly with a bow, their accuracy and speed was legendary.

Finally, the planes of Varith merged with the borders of the Great Forest. Alinar could feel the power of the land and the forest renew his strength. The two thousand six hundred and forty-two gold and white armoured elves came to a standstill. The light was fading, and the night sky was clear. The largest of the three moons had crested the horizon and was bathing the woods with its pale blue light. Thousands of stars twinkled as the sky started to darken.

"Hail to the forest," called Alinar.

"Hail the returning army," came a soft female voice. The low-hanging branches of the trees parted as a steady breeze blew from the forest, and out stepped a slim blonde female elf. She wore a simple long white dress that shimmered in the moonlight. A small silver circlet adorned her head and her feet were bare but no sound could be heard as she walked from the forest.

Alinar smiled as the girl approached. "Greetings, Daughter, I hope all is well."

The girl bowed her head. "All is well, Father," said Princess Almera. "The forest sensed your presence and the return of its children."

"Not all of her children are returning," replied Alinar sadly. "We have been gone far too long from our home."

The elven army continued its silent march into the forest. Almera linked arms with her father as they entered the forest.

"Tell me of the battle, Father, and of your journey home."

Alinar sighed. "You know I do not like speaking of the ways and wars and of men. But it was a necessity that we joined them, for should Sagoth had been victorious the war would have come to our lands and we would have faced annihilation. It was better to align our forces with King Tyrin now than to try and standalone against the might of the orc armies."

"And how is the king?" asked Almera.

"Why are you so fascinated by the humans?" asked Alinar, looking down at his daughter.

"They intrigue me," she replied. "Their lives are over so fast, yet they still find time to wage wars with one another, and yet they still can accomplish beautiful works of art and show great compassion."

"Tyrin has asked that we trade between our peoples."

"And did you agree?" asked Almera, barely able to hide the excitement in her voice.

Alinar smiled at his daughter. "One step at a time, dear heart. First, I must call upon the wisdom of the elders and apprise them of what has transpired."

It had been a month since Corporal Mendez had arrived back in the city, the king had now dined with the trader's daughter four times now and had scheduled another meeting with her tonight. Her father had grown quite pompous and had taken to calling the corporal by his first name, forgetting his rank.

Derrel swore under his breath as he slid his black boots on in readiness for his morning patrol, "Pompous fat wind bag! If I hadn't stopped in the market that day, you would still be just a fat old wind bag selling your fruit."

Tal burst through the door.

"Who are you talking to?" asked the young squire.

Derrel looked at his younger brother, his face was flushed, and he was out of breath. "No one," replied Derrel. "And how many times have I told you to knock?"

"Sorry," replied the youngster. "I just thought you should know that a ship has been spotted in the harbour flying the duke of Movale's coat of arms."

"And?" asked Derrel.

"Well, I was in the kitchens this morning, stealing a fresh loaf, when I heard one of the cooks say that she'd heard from a servant who'd overheard Father taking to one of his sergeants that a raven had arrived a few days ago. It was carrying a note to father from the duke. It seems that watch captain you hit is a cousin to the duke and he has petitioned the king for his captain to fight you in a duel."

"Ristus be praised!" said Derrel, invoking the God of Battles' name. "Go to Father and find out if this is true and if so, tell him I accept."

Tal set off to go, but his brother grabbed him by the back of his grey tunic. "Don't tell Father you were stealing from the kitchens again."

Tal smiled. "I've only been caught once and the punishment was eight hours in the stocks with no supper, but that night, I ate like the king. The cook's daughter fancies me," said Tal, laughing, and disappeared out through the door.

Duke Cedric Tybost had never enjoyed travelling by ship, even the short journey across the trapped sea to the capital turned his stomach. The duke was a large man with a thinning head of mousy brown hair, he was given to expensive taste. Over the years, he had dined on the finest foods and wines which had contributed to his spreading gut. His cousin Kainos Tybost had come to him early one morning, blood streaming from a broken nose, both eyes were blackened and his two front teeth were broken.

Kainos had told his cousin of the eleven armed men riding through the streets early that morning and how they had shown no respect to the laws of the duchy. The duke had tried to explain to the captain that one of the men had been the king retuning from the battle of Black Mountain.

"How was I to know that, cousin?" shrieked Kainos. "If the king had identified himself to me, I would have escorted him to the harbour."

"The king does not need to identify with anyone, cousin," said the duke. "He is the king."

"This is not about the king now," wined Kainos. "It's about

honour, my honour. That corporal hit me in front of my men, knocking me off my horse. Look what he's done to my face." The captain's voice was shrill.

The duke had relented and finally sent the raven, asking the king for the duel. He had demanded that honour needed satisfying and that the young corporal had acted without honour. The answer from the palace had arrived the next day, asking the duke and the captain to attend the palace post haste.

The ship finally came to a stop and the gangplank had been lowered to the dock. In the harbour, dock workers looked on in amazement as a large fat man dressed in outrageous red trousers and a blue silk shirt trimmed with white pearls stood at the top of the gangplank. His brown buck skin boots were made from the finest animal hide but what made him stand out the most was the purple velvet cloak draped round his shoulders.

Behind the large fat man stood a lean, brown-haired, hook-nosed, pocked face man dressed in black leather from head to toe, a silver hilted sabre hung at his left hip and his face showed fading bruising around both eyes.

Corporal Mendez had been summoned to the throne room. The young officer had changed his normal day-to-day uniform of black woollen trousers and black tunic to his official dress uniform of black leather trousers and a white cotton shirt that had been cleaned and pressed, the silver buttons down the front of the shirt shone in the sunlight. Corporal Mendez had tucked his ornate helmet under his left arm and his ceremonial sabre had been polished to a sheen.

Tal hurried behind his brother as they made their way down the corridor. Strapped to Tal's back was Derrel's arming sword, the blade was three feet in length, the guard was made from silver that swept around and away from the wielder's hand, the handle had been wrapped with black leather and was topped with a silver pommel bearing the king's coat of arms; two crossed swords encircled by a crown.

The sound of Derrel's boots echoed on the white marble floor as he quickly marched his way to the throne room. Servants hurried out of the corporal's way, ducking back through doorways or back down corridors as the corporal and his squire marched past. King Tyrin sat on his gold and ebony throne, his face showed his irritation at the fat peacock of a man sat to his left.

Tal noticed that the king's clothes of blue leggings and white shirt paled at the side of the duke's. The blue of the king's clothes matched the curtains and ornate rugs of the palace throne room. To the right of the king stood his father, General Kaylin Mendez, dressed as ever in his formal garb of black boots with black leather trousers and white cotton shirt. At the foot of the raised dais stood a man dressed in all black.

Derrel recognised the man as the captain of the watch he had struck. Corporal Mendez approached the dais and bowed low to his king.

"You wished to see me, Your Majesty?" asked Derrel.

"Ahh, corporal, thank you for coming so swiftly. Allow me to introduce the Duke of Movale." The brightly dressed man nodded toward the corporal and waved a lace handkerchief under his nose, causing the fat of his neck to wobble.

"Your Grace," said Derrel, bowing his head.

"And you remember the captain of the watch," said the king with a raised eyebrow.

"I do, Your Majesty," said Derrel, not taking his eyes from the king. "This is the man I struck as we were making our way through Movale, he had barred our way." The king held up his hand for Derrel to stop talking.

"Corporal Mendez," Tyrin began, "you are one of my finest soldiers and follow orders without question; therefore, I would like you to apologise to the captain and decline his request of a duel."

Derrel stiffened at his king's request. "As you wish, Your Majesty," said the corporal, bowing to the king. Derrel turned then to the captain. "My apologies, sir, I acted in haste and regret my actions and ask for your forgiveness."

"Captain Kainos," said Tyrin, "do you accept the corporal's apology?"

"I do not, Your Majesty," replied the captain. "He insulted my honour and the honour of my duke by striking me. I demand the duel stand." Kainos removed a black leather glove that was tucked in his belt, turned and faced Derrel and slapped Corporal Mendez across the face.

Tyrin stood and in a cold voice spoke through gritted teeth. "Captain, I urge you to withdraw your demand. Corporal Mendez is a fine swordsman and has apologised for his actions."

Kainos stepped forward and bowed slightly. "Your Majesty, I too am a fine swordsman and my challenge stands."

Tyrin let out a sigh. "Very well then, the duel shall take place tomorrow at noon."

Kainos interrupted the king. "Your Majesty, I am ready now and I'm eager to get this over with."

Tyrin fought back his anger. "Very well, Captain, the duel will take place in one hour in the courtyard. Is this agreeable with you, Corporal?"

Derrel bowed. "It is, Your Majesty," he replied coolly.

Chapter Six

Word had spread that Corporal Mendez was to have a duel in the courtyard. Soldiers were gathering round the ramparts, placing bets and waiting in anticipation to watch the corporal in action. Chairs had been placed for the king and duke at one end of the courtyard along with General Kaylin. A physician had been summoned to attend the wounded after the duel.

The black clad figure of Kainos stood awaiting the arrival of his opponent, the captain drew his sabre and started to move through a series of exercises to loosen muscles. The duke smiled as he watched his cousin spin and twirl.

Turning to the king, the duke nodded his approval. "He is quite the swordsman, wouldn't you agree?" asked the duke.

King Tyrin smiled. "Indeed, he is, but I would ask you to talk with your cousin to reconsider his challenge."

"I'm afraid that Kainos has made up his mind on the matter, Your Majesty; but there is another matter I wish to discuss with you, Your Majesty."

"And what would that be?" asked Tyrin.

"As you know I have two daughters of marrying age—"

A cheer went up from the gathered soldiers, interrupting the duke, much to the relief of Tyrin. Corporal Mendez walked into sight, followed by his squire. The young man had stripped his clothes from the waste up. The duke noted the lean muscular figure of the young corporal.

"A little risky fighting bare-chested," the duke said.

Tyrin smiled. "The corporal may be young, but he has had one of the best teachers in all of the kingdom, and he has won the garrison tourney for the last three years running."

Derrel turned to his younger brother and drew his sword from its scabbard.

Tal smiled at his brother. "His left knee has had an injury in the past. Look at how he drags it slightly when he turns."

"I've noticed, this will be over quickly," said Derrel, smiling. He turned to the king and held his sword in salute.

Tyrin stood. "Gentlemen, are you sure that this is what you both want?" he asked, looking directly at Kainos.

"It is," replied the captain.

"When this duel is over, I hope that this will be an end to this nonsense," continued Tyrin. "As this will not be a death bout, the winner will be the one who draws first blood; is this agreed?" asked Tyrin.

"Agreed, Your Majesty," replied Derrel.

Kainos merely nodded, but his irritation showed on his face.

"Then, gentlemen, let the duel commence."

Derrel turned and barely had time to block the sweeping slash from Kainos.

Derrel jumped back but Kainos ran forward, attacking with lightning speed, bringing his sabre down in an overhead strike. As Derrel blocked the cut, Kainos spun on his right heal, aiming his sabre at Derrel's mid-section. Derrel knew that if the blow had hit, his bowels would now be on the courtyard floor. The captain wasn't trying to draw blood, he was trying to kill the young corporal and would claim it had been an accident.

Again, Derrel blocked a sword strike that would have killed him if it had landed. Derrel knew he needed to end the duel and end it fast. Kainos lunged forward, aiming the point of his sabre at Derrel's chest, which the younger man blocked. With a flick of his wrist and a sidestep, Derrel pushed the captain backwards.

Derrel feigned an attack on the captain's left, causing him to overextend, which caused his left foot to slip, creating an opening. Derrel reversed his sword and brought the pommel up, hitting the captain in his face, breaking his nose again. Captain Kainos staggered back, blood running freely from his nose. A huge cheer went up from the gathered soldiers.

"Well played," said Tyrin, coming to his feet. "That was an excellent move, I declare Corporal Mendez the winner."

"No," screamed Kainos. "He cheated!"

"The move was fair; the corporal has drawn first blood that was stipulated at the start."

"But, Your Majesty," protested Kainos.

"I said the duel is over," shouted Tyrin. "Cedric, control your captain."

"Yes, Your Majesty," said the fat duke, struggling to get out of the chair.

"I demand the duel continue," shouted Kainos; his face flushed with anger.

"Cousin, please control yourself," pleaded the duke, still struggling to rise. Kainos let out a scream that sounded bestial.

"Look out!" shouted Tal.

Kainos slashed his sabre towards Derrel's neck; the corporal brought his blade just in time. Kainos continued to attack, his sabre a blur, hacking and slashing, but Corporal Mendez had an answer for every attack.

"Enough!" bellowed Tyrin, but Kainos didn't hear the command, his battle rage had taken control and he wanted blood. Derrel's sword skills were all that was keeping him alive. Captain Kainos was a fine swordsman, but he had not been trained by General Kaylin.

Derrel ducked under a wild slash and slammed his left fist into the captain's chin, causing him to stagger back once more. The captain ran forward, hacking in desperation, trying to break through his opponent's defence. Kainos now knew that he faced a far superior swordsman, and at least three times the corporal could have landed a death blow but had let the captain live; this only enraged Kainos, making him madder.

This youngster had not only insulted him, he now wanted to rob him of his pride, but all the captain had left now was his pride. Kainos had bragged to his men back in Movale that he would bring the corporal's head back and hang it from the gate of the city watch. Kainos circled the young corporal and made a desperate lunge, trying to stab him through the heart. Their swords locked together at the hilt.

"Stand down, man," snarled Derrel through gritted teeth.

"Not till you're dead," hissed Kainos.

Derrel pushed the captain back and brought his right leg up, kicking Kainos in the gut, causing him to stagger backwards and the air to explode from his lungs. Taking a deep breath, Kainos charged in, his sword held in an overhead strike aimed at the corporal. Derrel waited until the last second, then spun on his heal, sidestepping the captain's attack. He reversed his sword and slammed it through the captain's stomach as he charged forward, the blade exited through the captain's back. Derrel twisted the blade and dragged it to his right.

The blade cut easily through flesh and muscle as Derrel slid the blade, clear exiting it over his opponent's hip.

Captain Kainos took two faltering steps then pitched forward and hit the floor without a sound, his sabre clattered across the courtyard. All in attendance stood in stunned silence. \

It was the duke who spoke first. "You murdered him!" screamed the fat duke. "I shall see you hang for this."

"Nonsense!" thundered General Kaylin. "The corporal fought in self-defence; your man did not yield after first blood was drawn."

"I disagree," said the duke, his voice becoming high-pitched.

"Enough!" roared Tyrin.

The duke shrank back into his chair, holding his handkerchief to his mouth.

"General Kaylin is correct, the corporal could have landed the death blow easily. Your man was out-classed and humiliated himself, and you, my lord duke. Does the captain have family?"

"Yes, Your Majesty," stammered the duke. "He has two sons and daughter, and a wife."

"Well, then, my lord duke, you will carry a letter bearing my seal that states the captain disobeyed an order from the king, and by his own actions caused his death, and furthermore there is to be no blood feud against the corporal and his family. This I decree by royal order, is that understood?"

"Yes, Your Majesty," said the duke sheepishly.

"Good," said Tyrin, "then I assume that you will wish to depart for Movale with all haste. General, please see that the duke is escorted back to the docks and his ship. Send a raven to the harbour and make sure that the duke has a royal escort back to his lands."

"At once, Your Majesty," said General Kaylin, saluting.

"Now, gentlemen, if you will excuse me, I have plans for later on this evening." The king nodded his head to the duke and left.

"My Lord," said General Kaylin, offering a hand to the stunned duke. "If you will."

Derrel handed his sword to his brother. "Clean this and return it to my quarters."

"That was a risky move," Tal told his brother. "How did you know he would charge in like that?"

"His eyes," replied Derrel. "He was desperate to win, he knew I was a better swordsman than he was and knew I could kill him anytime I wanted to. He gambled everything on one move."

"If you were better than him," persisted Tal, "why didn't you kill him earlier?"

Derrel ruffled the boy's hair. "You heard the king, it was not a death bout."

"But you killed him in the end so why didn't you just kill him to start with?"

"I had to wait till he broke the rules. When he attempted to kill me, the law of the duel changed."

"I understand that," said Tal, "but—"

"Just take the sword back and clean it," said Derrel. The youth sighed and took the sword.

General Kaylin sat astride his mount on the dock side. The Duke of Movale's ship had set off on the short voyage across the trapped sea. The general had dismissed the accompanying soldier. An uneasy feeling sat with Kaylin as he watched the ship sail into the distance. His son had acted with honour during the duel and the king had ordered that no more blood would be spilt after the captain's death, but Kaylin suspected that the captain's sons would seek revenge somehow.

That evening, General Kaylin sat in his private rooms; the king had been entertaining the daughter of the market trader again. Kaylin felt a sense of relief that Tyrin had finally found someone to take an interest in. The king had been so busy these past ten years running his kingdom. Tyrin had been an only child; his mother had died during childbirth and his father King Tobin had been devastated and had never taken another wife. This had set the dukes and barons talking of the weakness of the Degarre bloodline.

Tyrin had no siblings and no heir. If Tyrin were to marry, this would quieten the dukes. the land needed peace now, not a civil war. The candles flickered as a breeze blew through the open window, the night was warm. Kaylin ran a hand through his greying hair. He needed to protect his son from any revenge attacks that could come. In combat, Derrel was the best Kaylin had ever seen.

"Better than me," he said aloud, but an assassin's arrow or poison; these were a worry to the general.

It had been a couple of months since the duel had taken place and it seemed to Derrel that his father was punishing him. Derrel had been stuck at the castle now while his unit had gone on manoeuvres to the mainland, dealing with outlaws that had raided the king's cattle on the planes of Varith.

Derrel had gone to his father and protested about being held back at the castle, but General Kaylin knew that he couldn't keep him confined forever. Then Tyrin had come to the general with the answer to his problem; a mission of importance which would see a military unit gone for over a year if not longer.

Kaylin had asked Tyrin's permission to send Derrel as the commanding officer, he had told the king of his concerns over an assassination attempt on his son's life, Tyrin had listened carefully and tried to reassure his old friend that his concerns were nothing and that the duke would carry out the royal command, forbidding the blood feud. But Tyrin had agreed to let Derrel take charge of the mission, easing the old fighter's worries.

Chapter Seven

Elazar had been searching the library archives all night. It had now been months since the battle in the Black Mountains. Kadius lay fast asleep on one of the red couches that were in the library. The fifty-five-year-old mage had been sleeping now for over two hours, his bold head cushioned on one of his arms. A light tapping came from the door.

"Enter," said Elazar.

The door opened, and a student came in, bearing a silver tray. Upon it, she carried two cups of honeyed tea.

"Good morning, Master," said the student.

Elazar smiled and gestured to one of the tables. The student placed the tray down.

"Will there be anything else, Master?" she asked.

"Yes, please ask Lady Davira to join us," he replied.

The student bowed. "Of course, Master." She turned and hurried off. Kadius stretched and yawned.

"Any luck?" asked the bald mage.

Elazar let out a small chuckle. "We have been searching now for months and we haven't even scratched the surface," replied the mage, gesturing at the rows upon rows of scrolls and books that were housed in the library.

"Why not summon Shamari back? She has the most experience concerning the dark arts," said Kadius.

Elazar shook his head. "No, she is needed in the east. I have communed with her; it seems that it is not only dwarves that populate this new land, but a race of elves has been discovered. Besides, it would take around six months for her to get here."

"More elves, that's all we need, contemptuous creatures," said Kadius.

The door to the library opened and Lady Davira entered, bowing her head to the two mages. Her long red-gold hair had been pulled to one side and was held in place by a golden circlet. Her blue eyes were complemented by the blue of her master's robes. Lady Davira was a beautiful woman; her pale ivory skin showed no signs of wrinkles. Davira had been blessed by her magic which had extended her life; she was now in her hundredth year but didn't look a day older than twenty.

"You sent for me?" asked Davira, smiling.

"Please join us," said Elazar, pulling a chair out for her. "As you well know, Sagoth was defeated but before he was defeated, he cursed Tyrin and his bloodline. I have been working tirelessly to find a way to stop the curse, but I have found nothing. The gem has been split and is guarded, but I fear it will one day become whole again."

Davira stood and started to pace around the table. "The gem is where Sagoth draws his power from, and the pieces seek to join back together."

"Yes, yes," said Kadius, "we know this. What's your point?"

Davira paused in her pacing. "Magic that counters each other have a diverse effect on one another. If the gem sensed magic that could harm it, surly it would react in defence to counter that magic."

"It could be worth a try," said Kadius, taking a sip of the honey tea.

Elazar looked at the other two masters and took a deep breath. He reached inside his blue robes and produced a small gold box and placed it on the table. Releasing the clasp on the box, he opened the lid. Inside lay a crystal-clear gem.

"By the gods, man," said Kadius, "you've been carrying that thing on you all this time."

"The gold helps dampen its power," said Elazar.

Davira walked over to stand behind Elazar. "I would suggest a search spell cast by the three of us," she said. "Our powers combined should be able to do the trick."

"Nonsense," said Kadius, standing. "Let's just take the dam thing round the room." As he spoke, he reached out his hand, gripping the gem.

"No!" screamed Elazar, but his warning came too late. Kadius' hand closed on the gem. Instantly, the room was plunged into darkness. The candles fluttered as Kadius was engulfed by shadow. The mage screamed out in agony. Books and scrolls were blown from the shelves, Elazar tried to focus on the screaming mage but was unable to see him through the swirling darkness.

Bright light shot forth from Elazar's hands as he spoke the words of power. The light spell hit Kadius, throwing him through the air and sending him into a stacked shelf of scrolls. The gem fell from his hand and skittled across the floor. Davira grabbed the small golden box and scooped the gem inside, being careful not to touch it. She snapped the lid shut. Kadius moaned from under the pile of scrolls. Davira ran to his side and offered him a hand.

"Are you OK?" she asked.

"I'm fine," answered Kadius, standing and smoothing down his blue robes, brushing the dust from them.

Davira looked at the scrolls scattered around the floor. The parchments had blackened, all except for one. Davira bent down and retrieved it; she could feel a pulsing energy coming from the scroll.

Kadius looked over at his friend. "Did you have to hit me that hard with the spell?"

"Sorry," said Elazar, "but I had no choice, that thing," said Elazar pointing to the golden box, "would have destroyed you."

"I think you did the right thing," said Davira, interrupting the two mages.

"I'm glad you think so," said Kadius, giving her a pained look and rubbing his head.

"No," said Davira. "It worked look! She handed Elazar the scroll.

The mage opened it and read the script.

"One born of innocence and pure of heart, shall have the power to resist that which is dark, for the touch of the innocent's hand shall shatter that what the demon must demand."

"What does that mean?" asked Kadius. "It makes no sense."

"It's a start," put in Davira.

"So, all we need is an innocent to stop the curse," asked Kadius. "And how do we find such a person?"

"It's not that simple," said Elazar. "It says one born, that person may not have been born yet. Some of these scrolls are hundreds of years old, they date back to before Ebras was the master mage, and some are just the ravings of mad men that claimed to be oracles or prophets. Some are prophecies that have come to pass, others that are prophesised yet to come true. I know of one way never to let Sagoth come back; I must go and see Tyrin immediately."

Elazar picked up the golden box. "One of you must take this and seal it in the north tower, place it in the highest room and cast a ward spell."

"I'll do it," said Kadius, stepping forward. "It's the least I can do after what just happened."

Elazar handed the golden box to the mage, then turned to Davira. "Please stay here and see if there are any more writings or references to the innocent one mentioned in the scroll."

Davira nodded. Elazar raised his hands, spoke the words of power and vanished from sight.

The day had started without incident and Tyrin was looking forward to another evening where he would be joined by Emelia. The king had grown quite fond of the trader's daughter over the past few months. He chuckled to himself, what would the local dukes and barons with eligible daughters say? All of whom wanted to link their houses to the king's, how disappointed they would all be when Tyrin announced his betrothal to Emelia, the daughter of a market trader.

Tyrin smiled at the thought. Turning his attention back to the day at hand, the king would hold court today and pass judgment on several minor complaints. Picking up the papers off the oak desk in his private study, Tyrin quickly looked through them. One of the complaints was from a local noble who had claimed that his prize garden had been ruined by his neighbour's pet goat. The goat had slipped its tether and had gotten into the noble's garden and eaten most of the flowers.

The second complaint was from one of the stone masons. It seemed that the noble whose garden had been eaten by the goat had not paid the stone mason for repairs done to his house. The list went on and on like this; small and petty complaints that could and should be dealt with so easily but would now take up most of Tyrin's day.

The king sighed and placed the papers down on the desk. It

was days like this that Tyrin hated. People could be so petty with one another, it was probably the stone mason that had set the goat loose as revenge for not being paid by the noble.

A light tapping came from the door.

"Enter," said Tyrin.

The large oak door opened slightly, and a young maid peeped through. "Sorry to disturb you, Your Majesty," she said, "but there is a man here to see you."

"Tell him he will have to wait his turn like the rest of them who have a complaint," replied Tyrin.

The maid looked nervous.

"Begging your forgiveness, Your Majesty," said the maid in a timed voice, "but the man is most insistent."

Tyrin looked at the fear on the maid's face. "Who is this man to demand my attention?"

The maid stepped into the room and bowed. "He said his name is Elazar from High Castle. He just appeared in the middle of the court room and demanded to see you."

Tyrin thanked the maid and sent her to fetch in the mage. The oak doors to Tyrin's chambers swung open as Elazar strode through. With a wave of his hand, the doors shut firmly behind him. Tyrin could feel his anger rising as the mage stood in front of him. His black hair and beard were neatly oiled, and his blue robes were neatly pressed.

"To what do I owe the pleasure, Master Mage?" asked Tyrin, bowing his head.

"Let's dispense with the formalities, Tyrin," said Elazar. "We need to talk of Sagoth's curse and the gem piece you have. I was a fool to think we could contain its power by separating it, I have just witnessed what one piece can do to a powerful mage. I must have the pieces back, and I will hide them; only a being of power has any chance of resisting the evil that lies within."

Tyrin walked back to the oak desk and poured wine from a golden jug into two goblets and handed one to the mage. "When Sagoth fell, we all pledged to guard the gem pieces with our very lives, we all swore to this and now you want us to break our oaths. That demon's blood still stains the steel of my sword."

Elazar took a sip of the wine, it was sweet and flavourful. "You don't understand what you are dealing with," persisted Elazar. "The power that the gems have is unmeasurable, the darkness is seeking a new host. It wants to be whole again."

"I understand more than any," said Tyrin, "it was I who was cursed, it is my blood line that has to bear this and you have a hundred years to figure this out."

Elazar sat in one of the padded chairs that lined the wall of the king's private chamber. "There is a way," said the mage.

Tyrin gave him a quizzical look. "Speak on," said Tyrin.

Elazar took a long drink from the goblet. His blue eyes locked to Tyrin's.

"Do not sire any children; if your blood line ends with you, then Sagoth's curse can never come true." Elazar watched the colour fade from the king's face.

"Do you know the magnitude of what you ask?" thundered Tyrin.

"I do," replied Elazar.

"No, you don't," roared Tyrin, slamming his fist down on the oak desk. "The line of Degarre brought order to this land, it was my bloodline that forged this kingdom, my ancestors built this palace. Without an heir to my throne, the land would fall into chaos, civil war would break out between the nobles. You ask too much."

Elazar stood. "I saw the fall of the eastern mountains, I

watched as your ancestors built this palace and I watched the city spring up around it. I have walked these lands for a millennia, do not seek to lecture me about your bloodline. What I ask of you, Tyrin, is the only way to ensure this kingdom's future."

Tyrin turned away from Elazar. "I cannot grant your request," said Tyrin, his voice calm and steady. "I have already chosen a bride and tonight I will ask her to marry me."

"Then you have doomed us all," said Elazar, placing the goblet on the table. Elazar turned to leave.

"Wait," said Tyrin. "If you want the gem, it lies in the deepest dungeon. It has been buried under five tonnes of rock and mortar. Take it if you must."

"No," said Elazar, "that burden lies with you and your choice. I have given you the answer to the problem we face; it will fall to you and your kin to prevent what has been set in motion."

Without a backwards glance, Elazar opened the doors and left. From the back of the room, an oak panel moved and slid to one side. General Kaylin stepped out from the hidden room.

"You heard?" asked Tyrin.

"I did, Your Majesty," replied the general, sliding the panel back into place.

"And your thoughts?" asked Tyrin, looking at his oldest friend.

"The mage has a point," said Kaylin. Tyrin was about to speak but his general cut him off. "You are right, Your Majesty, your ancestors brought peace to this land and a Degarre needs to be sat on the throne." Tyrin relaxed and poured another goblet of wine, offering one to Kaylin. The general accepted the goblet. "Can I ask, Your Majesty, why you told the mage we had buried the gem in the dungeon?"

Tyrin drained his goblet. "If Elazar thinks the gem is in one place, he will not go looking for it. He now believes it to be out of reach and that it cannot corrupt anyone."

"And if he learns the truth?" asked Kaylin.

"Only you and I will ever know the real location of the gem. If the gem is not here and someone comes looking for it, they can never find what is not here," said Tyrin, smiling. "Is everything in place like I asked?"

"It is, Your Majesty," replied Kaylin. "My son will lead the mission, I will oversee the departure of the ship myself."

"Excellent," said Tyrin. "Now to matters of the state." The king gathered up the papers from the oak desk and headed off to pass judgement on the complaints of his subjects.

The newly promoted Sergeant Derrel Mendez stood on the dock side watching the final cargo being loaded on to the ship. His father had asked him to undertake the mission to the new continent of Rainoa.

Finally, his father had released him from his watchful eye, the autumn morning air was fresh and a light breeze whipped at the sergeant's black cloak, his silver breast plate shone in the morning sun. Derrel had been given the king's flagship for the mission. It was the finest ship in the entire fleet, it boasted three huge masts, atop of the central mast flew the king's banner and two swords encircled by a crown.

The ship was over three hundred feet in length and had a crew of forty fighting men. Sergeant Mendez had hand selected fifteen of the best men from his unit to join him on the mission.

The sergeant had been at the docks since first light, supervising the loading of the cargo. The elderly cleric tapped him on the shoulder.

"Excuse me, Sergeant," said the weasel-faced little man.

Derrel turned to look at the cleric who was dressed in dirty tan-coloured leggings and a grey woollen tunic. He had a brown leather apron on which had stains from his breakfast down the front of it. He was now starting to annoy Derrel.

"You must have enough water for each man per day, each man consumes over three litters per day, then there is the food for you and the crew," the little man continued to rabble on.

Derrel listened but wasn't paying attention; he was distracted by the little man's wispy grey hair that was blowing in the breeze. the wind had moved the man's hair, revealing the bald spot that the cleric had tried to hide.

"Are you listening?" asked the cleric.

Derrel fixed his gaze on the little man. "Just have the ledger in my cabin with the daily intake for each crew member, I'm a soldier and I can follow instructions to the letter."

The cleric's face flushed red and he was about to protest when the sound of hooves echoed on the cobbled streets. Both men turned to see the king riding his grey stallion, flanked by General Kaylin and a squad of soldiers. Shadow's hooves echoed on the cobles as the great stallion pranced towards the dock. The little cleric bowed as the king approached and Sergeant Mendez snapped to attention.

"Stand at ease," said the general, dismounting from his chestnut mare. Derrel relaxed and looked at the king; he looked resplendent in his blue silk shirt and matching blue wool leggings. His pale blue cloak fluttered in the breeze.

"Your Majesty," said Derrel, bowing low. "You honour me with this mission, and your presence here today."

Tyrin nudged his mount forward. "Sergeant Mendez," began the king – Derrel felt a sense of pride at hearing his newly promoted rank – "this mission is of the upmost importance. I want you to establish a trade with the new continent and its dwarven inhabitants. We already trade with the dwarves of Grey Mountain, and I would like there to be a similar trade between us and this new land."

"It will be as His Majesty wishes," said Derrel, bowing once more.

"Good," said Tyrin, waving forward a soldier who was carrying an ornate wooden box. The box was a metre long and half a metre wide. The soldier stopped in front of the sergeant and opened the lid of the box to reveal a beautifully crafted golden dwarven war hammer laid on a bed of purple velvet. The shaft had been inlayed with jewels.

"Please present this as a gift to the dwarven leader as a mark of respect and a show of our intentions of trade."

"It will be as His Majesty instructs," said Derrel, bowing once more.

The soldier closed the lid and stepped past Derrel and proceeded to the gang plank and onto the ship.

"I wish you all the best in this mission," said the king, turning his mount. The grey stallion started to prance, his iron shoes striking the cobbled stones of the dock. "General, please join me back in my private rooms when you have said your farewells to your son," Tyrin called back over his shoulder.

"Yes, Your Majesty," answered General Kaylin as the king headed back towards the opposite docks of the trapped sea.

General Kaylin looked at his son and felt a sense of pride. His son looked every part of an officer in his black and silver uniform that matched the general's.

"I want you to take care while you're gone and don't let that gift for the dwarf leader out of your sight."

"You can count on me, Father," said Derrel.

"I sense a question coming," said Kaylin. "So, ask it."

Derrel straightened. "The sailors that returned from Rainoa reported that gold and silver were in abundance over there, and that the dwarves valued steel more. When that ship returned, the sailors had stripped every available piece of steel from their ship. The captain is now one of the richest men in Carthage so why would King Tyrin send them a golden hammer?"

Kaylin smiled at his son. "Just deliver the gift and give them Tyrin's trade terms."

"Yes, Father," replied Derrel, saluting the general.

The cleric had been stood to one side, patiently waiting and watching the ships being loaded. The final crate of food had been loaded on to one of the two supply ships that would follow the flagship on her voyage.

"Excuse me, sirs," said the little grey-haired cleric, "but I need your signature on the ledger, Sergeant."

Derrel took the feather quill, dipped it into the ink and signed.

"Thank you," said the little man. "You are all set to leave."

Derrel turned to his father. "Well, I guess I'll see you in a year if all goes well."

Kaylin took his son in an embrace. "Be careful," said the general.

Derrel smiled at his father and then headed up the gangplank. As he neared to the top, he turned, "General," shouted Derrel, "take it easy on Tal. He's a good lad, he just needs discipline."

Kaylin smiled and waved as his son boarded the ship.

White gulls dived and swooped as the ships made their way from the harbour to the open sea.

Derrel stood on the bow of the ship as she cut through the

waters of the eastern sea. The voyage would take over six months just to reach Rainoa; it would be a year or more before he would see Carthage again.

Derrel felt a stab of pain as he thought of his brother, he would miss the youngster and God only knew what kind of trouble he would get himself into without Derrel to keep an eye on him.

"Hoist the sail," came the shout from the captain. Men scrambled about the ship carrying out the captain's orders.

Derrel looked over to where the captain stood, he had one hand on the ship's wheel, with the other hand he would point at a sailor and bellow out his instructions. All the crew wore the dark blue cotton trousers and white cotton shirts of the king's navy, but the captain boasted a blue coat made of wool atop his white shirt.

His brown hair had been pulled back and was held in place by a leather throng at the nape of his neck. The captain looked to be around forty years of age, thought Derrel, his tanned skin showing lines and wrinkles of someone who spent most of their life under the sun.

Derrel made his way to stand beside the captain.

"All is well, Sergeant," said Captain Renshaw in his gruff voice. "We have a good tail wind, and the sea is calm." The captain's brown eyes constantly darted around the ship as if he was trying to watch everyone and everything at the same time.

"Secure that damn line," he bellowed. "Excuse me, Sergeant," said the captain, releasing the wheel and walking off.

A crew member ran forward to take the wheel and smiled as Captain Renshaw walked off, shouting at two crew members.

Derrel walked down the steps and headed to his cabin. Derrel looked at the cabin that would be his for the voyage, it was eight-feet wide and twelve-feet long with two portal windows which let in very little light. At one end of the cabin sat a single cot bed, upon the bed sat the ornate box for the dwarf leader.

At the side of the bed was a wooden desk and a small stool. Derrel pulled a flint and striker from his pocket and lit the two lanterns. Lifting the box from the bed, he placed it on the desk, then he removed his breast plate and cloak. Finally, he removed his boots.

It was going to be a long voyage. Walking to the bed, he stretched out his arms and dropped to the soft mattress.

"Ouch," came a muffled voice from under the bed.

Derrel jumped to his feet. "Who the hell is under there?" he snapped. A hand slid from under the bed, followed by a booted foot. Derrel reached down, grabbing a hold of the hand and dragged the person out. Tal stood in front of his brother with a mischievous grin on his face, his grey woollen jerkin and leggings were covered in dust.

"What the hell are you doing here?" snapped Derrel. "Father will be furious."

Tal was brushing the dust from his clothes. "He's going to be furious with me anyway; I got caught stealing from the kitchen again this morning," said the youngster.

"How many times have I told you to stop doing that?" snapped Derrel. "You've been caught before, why not just do your time in the stocks?" Tal shifted nervously. "What aren't you telling me?" asked Derrel,

Tal looked at his brother. "It was the king's breakfast I stole," he said, trying to look innocent. Derrel's hand flashed up, slapping the side of his brother's head. "Ouch! That hurt," protested the youth.

"Are you crazy?" asked Derrel. "Of all the stupid, idiotic

things to do, you go and steal the king's breakfast?"

"I didn't know it was the king's," said Tal. "It was only after I was caught and the cook shouted at me that I knew it was for the king. It just looked so tasty," he said, smiling. "The bacon was cooked to perfection, I knew you were taking the voyage and that you'd be gone for a while, so I thought the safest place would be here with you. Besides," added Tal, "I am your squire, and you forgot your arming sword," said Tal, diving back under the bed and pulling out Derrel's sword.

Derrel snatched the sword from his brother. "I didn't forget it," he said, "I couldn't find it."

"Exactly," said Tal. "You couldn't find it because I'd done what any good squire would do, I had it here ready for you." Tal smiled weakly at his brother.

"Well," said Derrel, "it's too late now to turn the ship around, but I need to release a raven and let father know where you are."

"No need," said Tal, "I left a note. He'll find it."

"OK then," said Derrel. "If you're staying on this ship, you're going to be put to work." The youth smiled. "But no stealing," added his brother.

Chapter Eight

Kadius ran down the dark corridor, the walls of grey stone were smooth and seamless under his hand as he ran on blindly.

The voice came again. "I can help you, I can give you what you desire."

Kadius turned, but no one was there. The voice came again; it was soft and welcoming. "Take up the heart, make me whole again and I will give you eternal life."

"No," screamed the mage. He turned once more and began to run, using the wall to guide him in the darkness. The floor suddenly fell away, and he found himself falling.

Kadius sat up in bed, the dreams had become more intense and had started after he had touched the gem. He had taken the gem to the north tower as Elazar had instructed.

The mage had left the library and had made his way through the castle grounds, coming to the entrance of the north tower. Kadius had caught his reflection in a bronze mirror. The normally grey stubble of his hair around his ears had turned black. He looked more closely, the crow's feet and wrinkles around his eyes were smoother. Kadius had then taken the steps two at a time to the top of the north tower. When he reached the top, he paused. Normally, he would be out of breath and his legs would ache from the long climb, but this time he felt nothing. He had stood at the door with the golden box in his hand and had every intention of carrying out Elazar's order to seal the box in the room, but no matter how hard he tried, he could not release his hold on the golden box.

The mage had tucked the box inside his robes, then he had performed the ward spell on the room. It had been a simple spell of concealment, any who came looking for the room would not find it. Kadius had changed the door to look like the stone of the wall, then he had placed a confusion spell that would make anyone who came looking for the room forget what they had come looking for. It was a simple rouse.

Kadius swung his legs from the bed and stood naked in his private chambers. The mage walked to a wooden desk in his room and opened a small draw. Inside lay the small gold box. With a shaking hand, he removed the box and placed it on the desk. Gently, he removed the clasp and flicked open the lid. Inside lay the gem, it no longer held its clarity; it had taken on misty sheen.

Kadius extended his arm and touched the gem with his index finger. Instantly, the mage felt energy flow through his body. No matter how much he slept, he never felt rested, only the gem would restore him. The gem pulsed with energy as the mage placed his finger atop of it. Begrudgingly, he withdrew from the gem and closed the gold lid. Turning to face the bronze mirror, Kadius gazed at his reflection and smiled. What looked back at him was no longer the balding middle-aged man. Instead, there stood a lean, dark-haired man who looked no older than twenty. He dressed in his blue master's robes and cast a spell of illusion, giving himself his old appearance, then he made his way out of his private rooms to join Elazar and Davira.

As the mage walked across the courtyard, most of the students were carrying out their daily duties that kept High Castle running. Kadius walked by students, and they bid him a good morning. The master mage smiled warmly back at them as he made his way to the library where Elazar had selected some of the more senior students to help find a way to stop Sagoth's curse from coming to fruition. Elazar had returned from Carthage after pleading with Tyrin not to sire an heir, thus nullifying Sagoth's curse. The monarch had refused Elazar, so now it had fallen to the magic users of this world to find a way to stop the curse.

Kadius entered the library. Some twenty students had been selected for the search but none had been told of the gem piece that Elazar had brought back to High Castle. All that had been told to them was they needed to find any reference to the destruction of the Black Heart Gem.

Davira approached Kadius as he entered the library. "We have had no more luck," she told him, "and I fear we have no other alternative than to prevent Tyrin from siring any heirs."

Kadius shook his head. "Elazar has forbidden us from interfering in any way with Tyrin and his bloodline; it must be Tyrin's decision."

"It would be so simple," said Davira, "I could cast a spell that would render his bride barren. No one would be harmed, it would be so easy."

"We can't," replied Kadius. "What if one of their children is destined to do great deeds? We could change the balance of destiny."

"Then I fear we must search this entire library," said Davira, sweeping out her arm at the enormity of the library.

"I can see that we have plenty of willing students," said Kadius. "If I'm needed, I will be teaching my lessons." He bowed to Davira and left.

For weeks, Kadius seemed to distance himself from the search in the library, he said the same thing every morning. "Well,

I must be off, my students can't teach themselves." This happened every morning; first, he would come to the library, ask of the progress and then quickly leave. At the end of every day, after he had taught his students, he would retire to his rooms and have a student bring his meal to him. The next day, he would appear, and the routine would start again.

On one morning, a few weeks after he had first touched the gem, Kadius failed to attend the library. That morning, one of the students came to Elazar and Davira.

"Excuse me, Masters," said the student, bowing, "but Master Kadius has not turned up to teach his class this morning. I have been to his rooms and a note was passed under the door to me."

Davira held out her hand and the student passed her the note. Once more the student bowed and left. Davira broke the wax seal on the note and read it to Elazar, the note bade them to attend Kadius in his room and to come as soon as the note had been read. Once Davira finished reading it, the parchment ignited into flames and burnt away.

"A little dramatic, wouldn't you say?" asked Davira.

Elazar chuckled. "He has always been the same. Have I ever told you how I came to meet Kadius?"

Davira smiled. "I have known you for more than a century and never once have you told me of how you found Kadius."

The two masters headed out of the library and headed off towards Kadius' rooms.

"It was about forty-five years ago," began Elazar, "I had been in the south-west lands near the Venticana ports when I felt magic being used; it was raw and untrained. I had come upon a small fishing village where I had stayed for the night. It was early one morning and I was preparing to come home when I found a young dark-haired boy skimming stones across a lake."

"What was unusual about that?" asked Davira.

"The boy was skimming the stones using his mind. When I asked him how he did that, he merely said I just tell them to move and they move."

"That's pretty impressive for a ten-year-old," said Davira,

"I agree," said Elazar. "I asked the boy to take me to his father where I explained what I had seen, the boy's father agreed for me to take him. Kadius had such power contained within him, I thought that he would have been blessed by his powers and that long life would have been his, but sadly he has continued to age."

The two master mages soon found themselves stood at the door to Kadius' rooms. The thick oak door was shut and no sound could be heard from within. Davira tapped on the door.

"Enter," came the familiar voice of Kadius, muffled by the thick door.

Elazar pushed the door, it swung open easily. The two mages were greeted by Kadius who was stood at the foot of his bed, upon which was a large travel pack.

"Are you planning a trip?" asked Davira.

"In some sort of way, yes," replied the mage.

"What's going on?" asked Elazar, looking round the room which had been cleared of all personal belongings.

Kadius seemed to visibly sag. "There is something I must show you both." Kadius raised his hands and muttered a word of power, dropping the illusion spell. Davira gasped, for what greeted her was a bent and twisted old man. The top of his bald head and hands were covered in liver spots, long wispy white hair hung from the side of his head that touched his shoulders. The old man staggered. Elazar stepped forward to help, but the old man held up his hand.

"No, my friend," said Kadius. "I'm OK, I must look worse

than I feel," he continued.

"What has happened?" asked Davira.

"It is the effect of touching the gem; it has been slowly draining me, my power is not as great as either of yours."

"Why didn't you come to me sooner?" asked Elazar.

"It would not have been of any use," said Kadius. "I can feel my life draining as we speak. I have used up most of my powers over the last few weeks trying to fight this, but alas my powers are almost gone."

"No," said Davira, tears running down her cheeks. "There must be a way."

The old man shook his head as he looked at the beautiful red-haired woman, who stood openly crying. "I ask one last favour," said Kadius.

"Anything," said Elazar.

"Do not search for me, I wish to die in peace sat on a mountain side, watching the sun set." The two other masters nodded their agreement.

"It will be as you wish, my friend," said Elazar.

Kadius smiled at them both. "Do not grieve for me, my lady," he told Davira. "We all knew this day would come."

"This is my fault," said Elazar.

"No, my friend, the fault lies with me. I was the one who held the gem, I should have sensed the evil that lies within. Just know that the accursed thing is locked away where it can do no more harm. Do not approach it, my friends, lest it corrupt you too. Leave it in the place of solitude that I placed it in so it may not harm another."

With a trembling hand, Kadius placed his hand on his pack, spoke the words of power and vanished.

Chapter Nine

Months had passed since the defeat against the armies of King Tyrin. Word had spread throughout the orc clans that Urag of the Bear Skulls had declared himself war leader of all the clans and was now amassing an army to defeat the humans and dwarves. Many of the other clan leaders had flocked to his banner. Urag was known for his fighting prowess, his clan was one of the largest and most powerful. Now he had taken charge of the other clans, demanding that the clan leaders pledge to him. Any who did not pledge their clan had to face Urag in single combat to the death. Those that took the pledge were made one of his captains.

The orcs had suffered huge losses during the battle, depleting their numbers. Urag knew there to be over a hundred different clans; some of them numbered in their thousands, others only numbered fifty or less. These were new clans or clans that had been attacked by another clan taking their territory and their females.

The amassing orc clans had made camp to the north of the Black Mountains where it bordered the swamps of Noras. There, they were safe from prying eyes; no one would see the gathering of the orcs. Urag sat on a roughly constructed throne of wood and bone, the other clan leaders stood to either side of him. Torches had been lit, casting shadows around the encampment, giving Urag's grey-green skin an eerie red demonic glow. Urag had stripped away his armour and sat only in a fur loin cloth, the muscles of his powerful frame on show for everyone to see. The leaders of newly arriving clans stood before the new orc war leader and his captains. Xruul stepped forward and pointed his square-bladed battle axe at a tall lean chieftain.

"Who are you and what is your clan name?"

The tall chieftain reached up and removed his helm that had a human skull as a face guard. "I am Rakgu of the Red Foxes. I have two thousand warriors to pledge to you, Great Urag."

Xruul gestured the tall orc forward and held out his battle axe. Rakgu placed his hand on the blade and sliced open his palm, then walked forward and placed his hand on Urag's chest. More and more chieftains came forward to repeat the blood oath.

It was close to midnight as Urag walked through the now-quiet encampment. Over seventy of the clans had pledged loyalty to him and now the goblins had started to flock to his banner. A noise came from his left; Urag's hand dropped to the hilt of his dagger. The small form of Mug limped from between the black tents and bowed.

"There is unrest in the camp, my leader," said the little orc. "Food is running low and tempers are rising, there is not enough game to hunt in the swamps and it will be weeks before the supplies arrive from the clans bringing in livestock."

Urag looked at the little orc. "Bring me Xruul, I will provide enough meat for all."

"How?" asked Mug.

An evil smile set across the mouth of Urag. "We will dine on the flesh of our enemies, I will send Xruul to the human settlements over the mountains. The flesh of the humans will feed the army that I will build, and that army will cleanse this land."

Lieutenant Carter Jackson stood on the ramparts of the small wooden fort, idly rubbing at the brown two-day-old stubble on his chin. He watched his thirty soldiers dressed in their armour disappear into the distance as they set off on their morning manoeuvres. The forty-five-year-old lieutenant turned and headed back down the steps and across the small courtyard of the fort. Hollowrock fort was located half a mile away from the town. The fort itself was not that impressive, it only had three buildings. A central watch tower, the soldiers' barracks and mess hall. The lieutenants' sleeping quarters were connected to the rear of the mess hall.

The lieutenant was a man who kept his men in top fighting form. Every day he would send them out on a five-mile run. When he had first taken the position at Hollowrock, Carter had gone on manoeuvres with his men every morning. Now, after two years, he had grown fat and lazy. When the battle had started against the orcs, Carter had been ordered to stay behind with his men to protect the town of Hollowrock. The lieutenant had felt relieved when the order came, his men on the other hand had not; they were all young and eager to spill blood as were all young soldiers. Carter walked over to the mess hall where he knew the cook would still be. Rubbing his sizable paunch, he laughed.

"I think I'll do an inspection of the men's equipment when they get back," he said out loud. "Maybe Baron Longshaper will come one day and see what a fine job I'm doing and promote me away from this shit hole of a town," he said to himself.

The day had been like any other day in Hollowrock; the soldiers had been on a five-mile run but then the fat lieutenant had done a surprise inspection of all the equipment. As punishment for one soldier having a gravy stain on his red tabard, the men had been told there would be a duelling contest. The offending gravy stain had landed on the baron's coat of arms; a white dove with a flower in its beak was the insignia of the Longshaper family. The duelling contest took place while the lieutenant sat and watched all while he ate a plate of cold meats and cheese. All the men were tired and to have to duel with each other was the last thing they wanted.

The sun had started to set, and the lieutenant felt his stomach rumble. He had been going through the supplies list needed for the fort in his quarters, and tomorrow would send that list of requirements to the baron. Carter pushed his chair back from his desk, stood up and brushed the honey cake crumbs off of his grey tunic.

"My stomach tells me it's supper time," he said, laughing. The smell of roasting meats drifted across the courtyard as the lieutenant made his way to the mess hall, he could hear laughter from his men as he approached the door. *If they have the energy to laugh, then maybe I need to work them harder,* he mused to himself. As he got closer to the mess hall, he could hear the conversations of the soldiers.

"Did you see his chin wobbling?" came a voice.

"Which chin?" someone shouted. Laughter boomed out once more.

"What if the baron came and inspected this fort?" said another voice, trying to imitate the lieutenant.

"You have a stain on your tabard, right on the baron's coat of arms," came a third voice.

Laughter filled the air as the men continued to imitate the lieutenant. He was about to enter the mess hall when he heard one man call for silence.

"Wait, wait," said the voice. Carter's hand was on the door handle. "I heard a rumour," said the man, "about our lieutenant; it seems that when we go on our daily run, old fat Carter goes into town to the local whore house."

"There's nothing wrong with that," shouted one of the men. "We all go there when we have the chance."

"I didn't say there was anything wrong with it, I just heard that the whores charge him double because he's that fat." Laughter boomed out again.

Carter felt anger rising in him. "I'll show these bastards," he said as he made his way over to his quarters. "Starting tomorrow, old fat Carter will be going on the morning run and I'll show these young ingrates how to use a sword. I won three tournaments before I took this post."

The sun had set, taking with it any warmth. This far north, the nights were still cool in the autumn, but Carter still stripped off his grey soldier's tunic and leggings that all soldiers wore. When they were off duty, looking at his reflection in the bronze mirror, he felt disgusted at what looked back at him. How had he let himself get so fat? All the anger left him at that point; his men were right.

"What happened to you?" he asked the reflection. "What happened to the sword champion, what happened to the soldier that saved his captain from the raiders?"

Raised voices snapped the lieutenant out of his sorrow, he could hear the men running and shouting. Quickly, Carter pulled on his leggings and ran outside. A young soldier came running towards him.

"Sir, the town is ablaze, and the alarm bell has been rung. The orcs are raiding again."

Moving quickly, Lieutenant Carter started bellowing out orders to his men. Carter looked to the north and saw black plumes of smoke rising in the night sky. In the distance, he heard the town's alarm bell ringing.

"I want every man out here in full armour and ready to march in three minutes." Turning on his heel, he disappeared inside his quarters and started to don his own armour.

The shrill cries of the orcs echoed through the streets, drowning out the cries of the towns people who were being gathered in the town square. The orcs were running from building to building, setting them a blaze. The attack had come from nowhere. This was not a simple raiding party come to steal cattle or raid food stores, these orcs had come in force and were intent on the complete destruction of the town of Hollowrock.

Mothers screamed out as babes were dragged from their arms and thrown back into the burning buildings. The elderly were butchered in their beds or as they tried to run. Any who could not make it back over the mountain were to be killed.

Lieutenant Carter led his men at a run towards the stricken town. Over the past few years, his men had chased off dozens of raiding parties, the orcs would turn tail and run at the first sight of the baron's men charging in. The battle horn would be blown, and the orcs would scatter. Lieutenant Carter was breathing heavy as he ran, his chainmail undercoat had rubbed his armpits raw where his fat hung over, and his red tabard had been stretched to its limit as he had slid it in place. He knew he looked ridicules, but he was determined to show his men that fat Carter was a man of pride and honour.

He would start by killing these damn orcs. He would not just chase them off, his men would see what he could do with a blade. Carter and his thirty men ran towards the town square. They had heard the shrill cries of the orcs, he had seen a few of them moving between the buildings as he and his men had run into the burning town, but none had tried to attack them.

They're too scared, thought Carter. He wasn't interested in the ones that were running away from him, he wanted to find the leader and kill him. As the soldiers ran into the town square, nothing could have prepared them for the horror that lay before them. Hundreds of orcs had gathered the population of Hollowrock in the town square. Carter noticed a few bodies lying in the street where they had been slain. Carter and his men watched in horror as an orc warrior pulled a babe from its mother's arms and tossed into the flames. Another woman seeing the soldiers tried to run forward but was seized by two orcs and dragged back to the amassing people.

Lieutenant Carter stood stock-still, his eyes were wide with shock. "Orders, sir?" came a voice from his left.

Carter turned to look at the young blond-haired soldier.

"What?" asked Carter.

"Orders, sir, what do we do?" repeated the soldier.

Lieutenant Carter Jackson pulled down the front of his red tabard and drew his sabre. Confidently, he took a few steps forward away from his men.

"My name is Lieutenant Carter of the king's army, these lands belong to His Grace Gyon Longshaper. Desist at once and my men and I shall let you live." The words were spoken with conviction and for a moment, Carter thought that the orcs would leave.

But then, a tall orc stepped forward, dressed in a white bear skin. The head of the bear sat atop the orc's head, giving him a demonic look in the fire light. In his hand, he held a square-bladed battle axe. He raised the axe then he spoke, but Carter didn't understand the words.

Two orcs ran forward to attack Carter, the lieutenant stepped forward to meet them. The first one fell, its throat slashed open. The second died as Carter plunged his sabre through its heart.

The orc leader roared his frustration, and three more orcs ran forward to attack.

Again, Carter blocked the first sword attack, slashing his sabre across the throat of the attacker. The second orc thrust a spear towards his mid-section. Nimbly, Carter twisted his body away from the spear thrust. He took one step forward and smashed the hand guard of his sabre into the face of the attacker. As the orc staggered back, Carter's blade swept up, severing its head from its body. The third orc ran in, swinging a club of oak that just missed Carter's head. Stepping forward, Carter crashed his forehead into the orc's unprotected face, smashing its nose. Carter stepped forward and rammed his blade through the stunned orc's chest, skewering its heart.

Carter pulled his blade clear and looked again at the orc leader and repeated his warning. Carter's vision blurred and he staggered, he placed his hand down to his side and felt something warm and wet. The spear thrust had caught him as he turned, the blade slicing the flesh of his side where his chainmail no longer fitted him. A slimmer man would have avoided the blade, but the years of eating and drinking had made Carter a sizeable target.

Cruel laughter came from the orc in the bear skin as he approached.

"You fight well, human, but look around you," said the orc, pointing.

Carter turned to see that he and his men were surrounded. The orcs that he had seen running between the buildings were not fleeing, they had been moving to the rear of the soldiers, cutting off their retreat.

The orc spoke once more. "Tell your men to drop their weapons and join the others." The orc pointed towards the towns people. Carter was feeling dizzy from the loss of blood flowing from the wound.

"Stand your ground, men," shouted Carter. "Let's take as many of these bastards with us as we can." Carter heard the sound of steel sliding from scabbards and smiled. The smile faded as that sound was replaced by the sound of steel hitting the ground.

Shrill laughter filled the night as the orcs watched the soldiers surrender their weapons; Carter's heart sank as his men dropped their swords and shields.

"You cowards!" stormed Carter. None of his men could meet his gaze. "I may be fat and lazy," he continued, "but I will die like a man, not a coward." Carter screamed a battle cry and ran forward, slashing his sabre at the bear-skin-clad orc.

Xruul brought his axe up to block the sword blade as the fat human attacked, again and again. Xruul was forced back from the ferocity of the attacking fat man, but Xruul had seen the wound in his side and knew that he would soon tire.

Carter stumbled, he knew his strength was fading. He had tried desperately to end the fight quickly, hacking and slashing at the orc, but now his strength had gone, and his opponent knew it.

Xruul blocked a weak attempted thrust that would have seen the sabre pierce his heart. Grabbing hold of the fat man's wrist, Xruul dragged him into a head butt that drove him to his knees. Xruul brought his axe up and over his head, driving the blade down in a murderous arch. Carter brought his blade up to block the axe.

The sabre snapped six inches from the hilt, the axe blade continued down and sunk deep into Carter's shoulder. Pain flared through his body as the axe was dragged clear. With the last of his strength, Carter rammed the broken blade into the orc's side. Xruul roared in pain and kicked the fat man in the chest.

Carter tried to rise, but he had no strength left. The last thing Lieutenant Carter Jackson saw was his men gathering up their weapons and charging the orcs.

Chapter Ten

Tal had not taken to life onboard the ship too well; there was nowhere to hide, no streets to run down or roof tops to hop between, and the soldiers were all so serious all the time. The only fun Tal had found was to gamble with crew on a night, but that had been short-lived when the spare knuckle dice Tal had hidden fell from his sleeve. It was only his fast reflexes that saved him from a beating, that and his brother coming to his aid.

The crew had calmed down once Derrel had made Tal pay the money back he had cheated from them. Tal had been put to work mopping the decks and handing out the daily rations for the crew and the soldiers. The thirteen-year-old staggered into his brother's quarters and flopped down on his brother's bed, face down. Derrel looked over from where he sat at his desk.

"That's my bed," he said, "yours is over there on the floor."

Tal let out a muffled cry of frustration and sat up. "This is torture," complained the youth. "I wish that I'd stayed behind now and taken the punishment."

Derrel laughed/ "It's been two months at sea. We haven't even covered a quarter of the distance and you're already bored."

Tal jumped from the bed and placed his brother in a headlock. "Come on, Derrel, there has to be something fun we can do. You spend half the day going through that ledger and the other half talking to Captain Renshaw and checking the cargo."

Derrel pushed back his chair and stood while his younger brother still hung around his neck. "OK, Tal," said Derrel. "I'm going to teach you how to fight."

Tal slid down from Derrel's back. "I already know how to fight," said the youth, sounding disinterested. "You just have to hit the other guy harder and faster than he hits you."

Derrel chuckled. "That's OK for life in the palace, fighting with the other squires, but what happens when someone pulls a blade on you or when an angry sailor you've cheated wants to beat the money out of you that you've cheated from him?"

Tal shrugged. "They have to catch me first," replied the youth.

"I saw that," said Derrel. "It's a good job that rigging was there, or they would have had you."

Tal smiled. "Look, Derrel, I'm fast and good with my fists, that's all I need—" Derrel's hand flashed up, slapping Tal across the face before he could finish speaking.

Tal looked shocked. "You're not that fast," said Derrel.

"What was that for?" asked the youth, rubbing at his cheek.

"It was to show you that I'm faster and you could be as fast as me with training."

"I am as fast as you," insisted Tal, anger sounding in his voice.

"Prove it," said Derrel, pulling a dagger from his belt and handing it to his brother.

"How?" asked the youth.

"Take the dagger and stab me."

"What?" asked Tal, sounding shocked.

"You heard me, now try and stab me."

Tal lunged forward the blade, slicing thin air where his brother had stood. Pain shot through Tal's wrist as Derrel twisted it down, causing the youth to release the blade. With unbelievable speed, Derrel's other hand swept out and caught the blade as it fell. Tal felt the point touch his throat.

The youth swallowed hard. Derrel smiled.

"Get some sleep and be on deck at first light. You can have my bed tonight so you're not tired in the morning." Sheathing the dagger back in his belt, Darrel left the cabin.

Tal stepped out onto the deck. The sun was already rising on the eastern horizon as the ship made her way through the choppy waters. Derrel stood upon the deck, dressed only in his grey leggings and boots. Tal noted the defined muscles of his brother's body. Derrel smiled as his brother walked towards him, hugging his arms to his body to fight off the morning chill.

"Good, you're awake," said Derrel.

"Barely," replied Tal, rubbing his eyes.

"OK," said Derrel. "I know you're fast, but we need to work on your strength as well as your speed."

"And how do we do that?" asked Tal, shivering.

Derrel nudged a small wooden barrel with his foot. "Pick that up and place it across your shoulders behind your neck, then squat to the floor and stand back up. Do that ten times and then run to the other end of the ship whilst carrying the barrel."

"Then what do we do?" asked the youth.

"We keep going until you drop the barrel," said Derrel.

"You can't be serious?" asked Tal, looking at his brother, hoping this was all some kind of joke.

Derrel picked up the barrel and started to squat. On the tenth one, he set off running. "Come on, Tal," he yelled. Tal picked up the barrel and started to squat.

For thirty minutes, the two brothers ran and squatted with the barrels until Tal dropped his and fell on to the deck, gasping for breath.

"Not bad," said his brother. "Now get up."

Tal pushed himself to his feet. "Are we finished now?" he asked, gasping for breath.

"No," replied his brother, placing the barrel down. "Now we climb." Derrel grabbed hold of a coiled rope and handed one end to his brother, then with a heave he tossed the rope twenty feet up into the air over the first yard of the lower mast sail. He then tied off one end to the ship's rail. Grabbing another length of rope, he repeated it once more.

Standing at the bottom of the rope, Derrel lifted himself, hand over hand, until he touched the yard sail. Then, very slowly, he lowered himself back to the deck.

"Come on, Tal, let's see how many times you can reach the top."

Tal managed to reach the top twice before he slipped from the rope; blisters had formed on his hands and a couple were bleeding.

Derrel smiled. "Go find the ship's medic and have those wrapped, then come back here and you can complete your duties."

"How will I mop and clean with my hands like this?" complained the youth. "And you said you would teach me to fight, all you've done is tire me out and hurt my hands."

"First, you need to be able to hold a sword before you can wield one. We need to toughen up your hands as well as your body. Now go and get your hands seen to and I will see you here in the morning."

"And if I don't want to?" asked the youth.

Derrel pointed to the rear of the ship. "It's a long swim back to Carthage." The tone in his brother's voice sent a chill through Tal.

"I should have done my time in the stocks," grumbled Tal as

he made his way to find the ship's medic.

The raven had come not long after the ships had set sail for Rainoa. General Kaylin had read the note from his son, informing him that Tal had stowed away onboard the ship.

"Call off the search for my son," said the general to the young soldier who had brought the message. "It seems my son has found his sea legs."

The soldier had saluted and left the general alone in his quarters. the old general smiled. "Well, Tal, at least with your brother watching you, maybe you'll stay out of trouble," he said to himself. Two months had now passed and the old general missed his sons.

The streets of Carthage were alive with excitement, the king would make an announcement today and rumours were speculating from one end of the island to the other on what it could be that the king would say. Most of the gossip had been that the king would announce he was to marry.

The docks of the island were filled with ships and boats bearing the flag and coats of arms of the nobles that had arrived. All that the populace had been told was that at midday there would be a royal announcement.

People had gathered outside the palace walls to listen. Inside, the dukes and barons had gathered with their families, even the fat duke Cedric Tybost had attended, and he looked more outlandish than ever in his brightly garbed clothes.

Trumpets sounded and the distinctive sound of marching boots striking the ground could be heard as a full company of the king's soldiers marched from the palace into the courtyard where all the nobles were gathered. Fifty soldiers, ten abreast and five rows deep, all dressed in black and silver, came to a standstill. The trumpet blew once more and the soldiers all in perfect unison parted into two columns of twenty-five men on each side. As they parted, King Tyrin followed by General Kaylin walked through the centre of the two columns.

"A little dramatic," whispered Tyrin to Kaylin.

"These are your men, Your Majesty, and you are the king, and you did want to get the attention of the attending nobles."

Tyrin smiled. "I think what I'm about to tell them will set their tongues wagging."

"Indeed, Your Majesty," said Kaylin.

"I'm in such a good mood that I'm not even bothered that Tal has escaped his punishment," said Tyrin, smiling.

Kaylin grimaced. "Oh, don't you worry, Your Majesty. I'm sure that Derrel will find plenty of ways to punish him, he will wish that he'd stayed behind."

Tyrin let out a little chuckle. "We were all young once, General. How many times did you catch me doing things I wasn't supposed to be doing? I think it was my antics that put my father into an early grave."

"Your father died of a weak heart; it was nothing to do with you," said Kaylin, more sternly than he meant to.

"Well, I think that if my father were still here, this would definitely cause him to panic." Tyrin came to stand in front of the gathered nobles. He could see the Duke of Movale and the Duke of Varith. Alongside him stood the Duke of Wroving, who was talking to the Duke of Jovale; behind them stood Baron Richart Flavian from the Venticana ports. Tyrin could have stood there for twenty minutes trying to list the names and places of everyone that had attended.

General Kaylin's voice boomed out. "My gathered lords and

ladies, it is my privilege to present to you King Tyrin Degarre, ruler of the lands of Sharr, protector of the realm, and it is his right by blood that he rules these lands. Let all in attendance acknowledge this." The nobles all started to clap as Tyrin bowed his head and thanked his general.

Tyrin cleared his throat. "My lords, I would like to thank you all for coming today, I know that the journey for some of you has been a long one, and I offer you my hospitality while you are here." Tyrin looked at the faces as he spoke; all were smiling at the thoughts of staying within the palace. "It is my greatest pleasure to announce that I have decided to finally take a bride."

The attending women started to whisper amongst themselves; most of the dukes and barons had daughters of eligible age and a great excitement was now apparent amongst the attending women.

On the walls, heralds were repeating what the king had said to the amassing people and great cheers were erupting as it was being announced.

"Please, my lords and ladies," said Tyrin, calling for quiet.

It was the Duke of Movale that spoke next. "Please, everyone, could we have calm? Our glorious king is about to tell us all which lucky girl will become our next queen." The fat duke turned and smiled at his portly wife and two daughters.

A nervous hush fell over the gathered nobles. Tyrin smiled at the fat duke who had a confident smug look on his face.

Tyrin's voice boomed out. "It is my great pleasure to introduce to you, Miss Emelia Jones of Carthage."

A gasp went up from the gathered nobles as a young beautiful woman with gold blonde hair, wearing a light blue silk gown, stepped forward from behind the soldiers. Emelia walked forward to stand beside Tyrin and bowed to the nobles. It was the

Duke of Movale who spoke first.

"Begging Your Majesty's pardon, but who is the good lady's father? I do not believe that I know which noble family the good lady comes from, I have never heard of her father." The duke's voice had an air of panic to it. A hushed mumbling was now going through the gathered nobles.

"You will not have heard of her," said Tyrin. "Her father lives in the city, he is a market trader."

"This is outrageous," stormed the Duke of Wroving. The elderly duke stepped forward, using his cane for support. "How can you marry someone who is not of noble blood?"

"Noble blood?" stormed Tyrin. "How can any of you say your blood is more noble than the next person's? Most of you here have inherited lands from your families. You are rich because of the taxes you receive from your lands and it is that money which has granted you your nobility, not your blood."

Angry voices started throughout the gathered nobility.

"Ladies and gentlemen," came the calm voice of Richart Flavian, "if I may speak." The baron eased his way to the front of the nobles. The baron was an elderly man, tall and thin. His green trousers and white shirt were finely made as were the brown leather boots he wore. Tyrin's eyes narrowed. "With His Majesty's permission?" asked the Baron, bowing slightly. Tyrin nodded his head. "It would seem that the nobility of this land are upset with your decision." Murmuring started but the Baron raised his voice to stop any interruptions, "And it would seem that the gathered nobles expected you to align one of their houses with yours as your father did with my house. As you all know," continued the baron, "my sister, may the gods bless her soul, only gave birth to one son."

"And that son," interrupted Duke Tybost, "is the king. Your

bloodline continues through our monarch so what is your point?"

"If you will let me finish, Your Grace," said the old baron. "I am the last of the Flavian bloodline. I have no sons or daughters to inherit my lands, and as the king said, money will be the defining factor in who will rule the barony when I'm gone. It will be the next richest man in Nerath who calls himself baron." No one spoke for a moment.

"It would seem that His Grace the Baron Richart has spoken some home truths," said Tyrin. "It was your ancestors who were the richest or the most powerful family of your lands, they claimed themselves duke or baron, but it was my family that brought peace to the realm, and it was your families that elected mine to rule."

Emelia who had stood silent throughout the heated exchange stepped forward and spoke. "My lords and ladies, believe me when I tell you that when His Majesty asked me to be his wife, no one was more shocked than I, but I will assure you all that I have grown to love His Majesty over these past few months and that a marriage of love is better than having one of your daughters forced into a loveless marriage."

Muttering spread throughout the gathered nobles and the look of disappointment showed on the faces of most of the dukes and barons' daughters.

Tyrin stepped forward and took hold of Emelia's hand. "The wedding will take place in one week's time. Those who wish to attend are more than welcome to take advantage of my hospitality. Those of you who have," Tyrin paused as if choosing his words carefully, "duties that cannot wait are free to leave if they wish." Tyrin inclined his head to the gathered families. "That will be all," he told them.

Tyrin then made his way back towards the palace. The

soldiers turned, formed ranks and followed after the king and Lady Emelia. Back in his private quarters, the king paced around the room while Emelia and Kaylin sat on one of the ornate couches.

"I think that went as well as expected," said Tyrin, looking directly at Emelia.

"It would seem, my love, that the Duke of Movale was the most upset by your announcement," she replied.

"Rightly so," said General Kaylin. "Duke Tybost has two daughters, both of eligible age, and he has turned down proposals from other dukes and barons for his daughters. Movale is the largest duchy and should Tyrin not sire any heirs, that would put the duke's family on the throne."

"May the gods be merciful," said Tyrin.

Emelia stood and kissed Tyrin. "If you will excuse me, my love, I wish to go and see my father."

"Of course," said Tyrin. "General Kaylin will arrange an escort for you."

"I suppose I'll have to get used to having an escort from now on." said Emelia, smiling at the general.

"That you will," replied the general, bowing.

Chapter Eleven

Kadius had closed his eyes and merely said, "Take me away from here." the sensation he had felt had been strange; it seemed that time had stood still. Elazar and Davira were stood in his room back at High Castle, then a darkness had surrounded him. When his vision cleared, Kadius found himself stood in the ruins of the Dark Fortress. He expected an attack at any moment, but all was silent. The fortress had been destroyed by the fires, its black walls showed the damage from where huge boulders had struck that had been thrown by catapults.

The fortress itself had taken a lot of damage; most of it had collapsed, ravaged by the fires. Reaching inside his blue robes, Kadius removed the golden box. He stared at his reflection in the lid, the illusion spell of the frail old man still held in place. Kadius chuckled. The spell had fooled Elazar the Master Mage of High Castle, the most powerful mage in the land of Sharr.

"Not anymore," said Kadius, opening the lid.

Inside, the gem pulsed with energy. Kadius removed the gem and felt the energy flow through his body. Instantly, the illusion spell fell away to reveal a young man in his twenties. His hair was jet black and his body felt powerful. Kadius looked down at his blue robes and touched the gem to the cloth, which started to darken, turning as black as the hair on his head.

"That's better," said Kadius.

"When you have finished," whispered a voice in his head, *"we must get to work."* Kadius dropped the gem.

"Who said that?" he asked.

The voice came again but seemed distant. *"Pick up the gem, you fool."* Kadius looked around nervously. *"Pick up the gem,"* came the voice again.

With a trembling hand, he bent down and retrieved it.

The voice sounded again, this time it was clearer. *"I have restored your youth and given you power."*

"Who are you?" asked Kadius, his voice trembling.

"I am Sagoth, and you are mine now, Kadius."

"No," said the mage, panic in his voice. "You were destroyed, the gem has been split."

Cruel laughter sounded in his head.

"Foolish human, I cannot be destroyed; I am the power eternal. The gem will heal itself as it has healed you. When you have collected the other pieces, then I shall be reborn."

Kadius stood shaking his head. "I won't do it; I will take the gem back to Elazar and he will find a way to stop you."

Laughter came once more. *"You are now bound to the gem. Should you not hold to it, you will age and wither within a day. Death will take you. That has always been your biggest fear; you have always envied the long-lived, now I have given you what you desired most."*

"No, you lie, the gem has awoken my true power, I do not need it or you." Anguish sounded in Kadius' voice.

"Very well," came the voice of Sagoth. *"Then I will show you."*

Pain flared through Kadius' body, his joints became swollen and arthritic. His black hair turned snow white and fell from his head. His back became bent and painful and the muscles of his body shrank to nothing. His skin hung loose and looked like old leather.

"No!" screamed the mage, falling to his knees. "I will do your bidding, I will do your bidding." Kadius wept openly, his tears falling to the floor.

"Good," came the voice of Sagoth, sounding triumphant. *"Now stand."*

Kadius stood, his youth had been returned once more. Tears still welled in his eyes.

"Open your robes," commanded Sagoth, *"and place the gem to your chest."*

Kadius did as he was bid and with a trembling hand, he placed the gem to the centre of his chest. Instantly, pain seared his chest as the skin started to blister and form around the gem. Kadius cried out as the gem disappeared inside his body.

"Now you are truly mine," said Sagoth.

Kadius staggered and almost fell. He ran his hand over where he had placed the gem, the skin felt smooth to the touch. He closed his robes.

"What is your bidding, my master?" asked the mage.

"My orcs have gathered at the far side of the mountains, but they alone are no match for the armies of men. You will go to them and seek out Urag, leader of the Bear Skull clan."

"But, Master," interrupted Kadius, "the orcs will attack and kill me."

"No, my pupil, they will do my bidding. The gem will protect you from attack. The orcs must be brought here and my fortress must be rebuilt. I will give you the power to cast an illusion spell that will hide the fortress, none will see what we are doing. The preparation for my return begins now."

For weeks now, Tal had turned up every morning and had been put through his brother's training. He could carry the water barrel for over thirty minutes without dropping it, and now he could reach the yard sail ten times before his arms gave out. Thick calluses had formed on his hands and the skin of his hands had toughened.

As the two brothers finished their exercise, Derrel walked to the ship's rail and picked up a long-bound piece of cloth. Tal drank greedily from the water barrel.

"Not too much," said Derrel, untying the throngs that bound the cloth.

Tal watched as his brother produced two wooden swords that were identical to Derrel's arming sword.

"What are those for?" asked Tal.

"These," said Derrel, twirling the swords expertly, one in each hand, "are how I will teach you to fight with a sword."

Tal laughed. "But they're made of wood. How am I supposed to hurt anyone with one of those?"

The wooden sword in Derrel's left hand flicked out, striking Tal on the elbow.

"Ouch!" exclaimed the youth. "That hurt."

The sword in Derrel's right hand flicked, striking Tal on the side of his head. "Stop that," shouted the youth. "It hurts."

"Then stop me," said Derrel, tossing the sword from his left had to Tal.

As the youth caught the sword, Derrel attacked, slapping his brother on the shoulder.

"That's not fair, I wasn't ready," said the youth, rubbing his right shoulder.

"Then stop me," said Derrel again.

Tal swung the sword, aiming for his brother's head. The clumsy attack was blocked by Derrel who flicked his blade and struck Tal on the knuckles, making the youth drop his wooden sword.

"Ristus' balls!" said Tal, shaking his hand.

Derrel laughed out loud. "You should not say the god of battle's name in vain for when you need to pray to him to keep you alive, he will remember how you taunted him."

"Stop hitting me so hard," said Tal, his anger rising.

"Pick up the sword and make me," said Derrel.

As Tal bent forward to recover the fallen sword, Derrel hit the back of his brother's head with the flat side of the wooden blade. Tal let out a cry of anger and charged his brother, swinging the sword wildly. Derrel side-stepped his brother, but left his left leg in place, tripping the attacking youth.

As Tal fell, Derrel's wooden sword lashed out, striking the youth across the backside. Tal hit the deck of the ship and slid on his stomach, his head colliding with one of the barrels. The wooden sword clattered across the deck boards.

Tal managed to get to his feet, but his eyes looked glazed over. He felt something hard poke him in the chest. Looking down, he saw the point of his brother's wooden sword in his chest.

"Never lose your temper in battle," said Derrel. "It is the quickest way to die. Only a berserker loses his temper and they are unstoppable and will kill all before them."

"How do you know I'm not a berserker," said Tal.

"Because, little brother, you are far too clever to be one. Now, let's continue."

For the next few weeks, Tal and his brother practiced every morning; first, Derrel would take his brother through the exercises, then they would practice with the wooden swords. The weeks rolled by, turning into months. Tal had not noticed the change to his body; the youth had started to develop muscle, becoming toned and lean like his brother.

Tal was learning fast, becoming skilful with the wooden blade. On the evening when Tal and his brother retired to the cabin they shared, Derrel would talk of fighting tactics and strategies. The next morning during practice, Derrel would attack his brother using the strategy they had discussed the night before. Tal was learning fast and becoming quite the swordsman under his brother's instruction.

Tal had performed his duties for the day. He had even talked Derrel into another sword-fighting lesson. This time, however, Tal had asked if they could use real blades. At first, Derrel had been hesitant on his brother's request.

"But I need to be able to fight with real blades," the youth had persisted. Finally, Derrel had submitted.

Tal had run off and returned a few minutes later carrying a sabre and Derrel's arming sword.

"Where did you get the sabre from?" asked Derrel.

"From Corporal Diddier," said Tal, tossing his brother his sword.

"This is no game," said Derrel. "One false move and someone could die or be seriously injured."

"I know," said Tal, pulling the sabre from its scabbard. "I promise not to hurt you, brother, don't worry."

Derrel raised an eyebrow and drew his sword and placed the scabbard to one side. Tal lunged forward, his sabre pointing straight at his brother's midsection. The blade was turned away with ease. Again, Tal attacked; his thrust was blocked once again.

"Remember your foot work," said Derrel, "you're dragging your right foot."

Tal said nothing and shifted his stance then lunged, his blade was paired but with a flick of his wrist, Tal brought his sword up and around his brother's defence. Brushing Derrel's blade aside, he stepped in, punching his brother in the face.

Derrel staggered back and smiled. "Nice move, you have been listening, now let's see how good you are."

Derrel narrowed his eyes and attacked. Tal's sword came up and blocked his brother's blade that had been aimed at his head; the speed of the attack was dazzling and forced Tal backwards. The sound of steel on steel rang out, catching the attention of the ship's crew. They all stopped what they were doing and started to watch the two brothers. Tal's arm was beginning to tire; for every attack he threw at his brother, Derrel had an answer for it.

Tal now knew that Derrel had been taking it easy on him when they practiced, which made the youth angry. How would he ever be as good as his brother if Derrel wasn't trying his best against him? Tal backed away slowly then lunged forward. He over extended the weight of the sabre and the momentum of his lunge carried him past his brother. Tal felt a blow to the back of his head, then he sprawled to the deck. Laughter from the crew drifted to his ears, rage threatened to overwhelm him, then he felt the point of his brother's sword touch the back of his neck.

"You made the same mistake again," said Derrel.

Tal turned over, his anger threatening to overwhelm him. "You've been holding back," he snapped.

Derrel sighed. "Yes, I have. I want you to learn, and look at how you're reacting. If you ended up on the floor every practice, you would soon lose interest. I'm teaching you the same way Father taught me."

Derrel reached out his hand to his brother. Tal pushed himself to his feet and pushed his brother's hand aside. He stormed off to the cabin he shared with his brother.

"OK, you lot," came the voice of the captain, "show's over. Get back to work."

Tal lay on his bed. What Derrel had said had been true; if Derrel had beat him every day and humiliated him every day, he would have soon been bored with the lessons. Tal heard footsteps approaching the door, he closed his eyes and pretended to be asleep.

Derrel looked down at his brother. "Tal," he whispered. "Tal, are you awake?" His brother did not answer. Derrel walked over to the small desk, pulled out the stool and started checking the ledgers.

Tal wasn't in the mood to talk with his brother so kept up the pretence of sleep. He could hear the crinkling of the paper as Derrel leafed through the ledgers and he heard the scratching of the quill as Derrel wrote down the daily corrections and adjustments to the ship's supplies. Sleep soon came to the youth.

Tal's sleep was a restless one; strange images ran through his mind.

He found himself surrounded by darkness. There was no up, no down, just darkness. He could hear someone or something moving within the darkness.

"Who's there?" he called out. His voice didn't carry very far, it seemed muffled by the impenetrable darkness.

Then a voice spoke to him. "I can give you what you desire, I can make you the greatest swordsman the world has ever seen."

"How?" asked Tal.

"Heal the heart," came the voice once more.

"What heart?" asked the youth.

Tal's body started to shake, then he heard his brother's voice,

as if it was coming from a great distance.
"Tal, what are you doing? Tal, wake up. Wake up, Tal."

Tal's eyes opened. He was stood in his cabin; his brother was shaking him and in his hands he held the golden war hammer.

"What the hell are you doing?" asked Derrel. Tal looked at his brother with no comprehension on his face. "Tal, are you listening to me, what's wrong with you?"

Tal placed the hammer back in the ornate box and turned to face his brother, he seemed to be in a sort of trance.

"Tal, are you awake?"

Talk shook his head as if trying to shake himself from a dream. "I was mad at you," said the youth.

"For what?" Derrel asked.

"Never mind, I just kept thinking to myself one day I will be better than Derrel, and the next thing I knew you were shaking me awake."

"You were stood with that hammer in your hand and talking as though someone was in the room with you."

Tal looked around the cabin he shared with his brother. "I don't remember anything," he replied.

Derrel ruffled his brother's hair. "Go back to sleep."

The three ships had been at sea now for six months. Tal stood upon the deck next to Captain Renshaw who had been teaching the youth how to steer the ship. The weather was growing noticeably warmer.

"How can it be so warm?" asked Tal. "Back in Carthage, the weather will be freezing at this time of year."

Captain Renshaw let out a little chuckle. "Well, lad, according to that captain that came back from this land, it's always warm even when its winter."

"How?" asked Tal. "That doesn't make any sense. When it's winter, it's cold."

Captain Renshaw ruffled Tal's hair. "It's to do with where the land is, my boy. I've sailed the sea near Carthage for most of my life and never would I have thought that there could be land this far away. The longest I've ever been at sea was three months and we noticed the weather was warmer the further southeast we sailed, now them chaps that was aboard that other ship nearly died of thirst. Only half of them made it back and I don't think they died of natural causes," said the captain, drawing his finger across his throat.

Tal's eyes widened. "Why would they do that?" asked the youth.

"The water," said Captain Renshaw. "They needed the water that's why we've had two supply ships following us."

"Land ho," came the call from the crow's nest.

"Where away?" yelled back the captain.

"Off the starboard bow," yelled back the sailor.

"Well, lad, soon we'll be on dry land," said the captain, seeing the excitement on Tal's face. Captain Renshaw nodded towards the crow's nest. "Go on, lad, go and look."

Tal's smile nearly split his face as he ran for the rigging and started to climb.

Derrel came on deck and made his way to stand beside the captain. "How long before we reach land, Captain?"

"Oh, I'd say at least four hours."

"Good, please keep me informed," said Derrel.

"I will, Sergeant," replied Captain Renshaw.

"I don't suppose you've seen my brother?" asked Derrel.

The captain smiled and pointed up towards the crow's nest.

Derrel saw Tal's legs disappearing into the nest.

"Have him come to my cabin when he comes down, I'll go brief the men."

The voyage had taken just over six months and one of the supply ships had exhausted it supplies and the other was running dangerously low, but now the long voyage was coming to an end. Sergeant Derrel Mendez stood in front of the fifteen men he had selected for this mission, all of them had fought at Derrel's side during the battle with the orcs and all had proven they were men to be counted upon.

The men had all dressed in their uniforms of black leggings and jerkins adorned with the silver breast plate which shone in the midday sun.

"The men are already for your inspection," said the newly promoted Corporal Nikhil Didier, a young blond-haired man of nineteen years.

Derrel nodded his thanks to the corporal. "As you know, men, the king has entrusted us to open trade with this new land," began Derrel. "The dwarves here should be pretty much like the ones we've seen back home, the only difference is that gold and silver here is not as valuable as it is back home. As you will all have heard, the dwarves here value steel more than gold."

A smile crossed the men's faces. "I will, however, be carrying out a full inspection of every man returning home and you all will be expected to present your full royal amour." Grumblings came from the gathered men.

"The sergeant is speaking," roared Corporal Didier. Instantly, the training of the men kicked in and silence fell across the soldiers.

"The king knows that this voyage has taken you away from

your homes and your families," continued Derrel. "That is why you will receive one year's extra pay in full when we return to Carthage." The smile returned back to the men's faces. "Now none of us have set foot on these lands before and we do not know what we will face once we get there. All the information we have has come from Lady Shamari of High Castle. She has been here for over a year now and she has informed His Majesty that the dwarves are protective of their lands. This land and its customs are alien to us, so I want you all to act as if your life depends on it. Is that understood?"

"Yes, Sergeant," came the reply from the men.

Chapter Twelve

Captain Renshaw glided the ship expertly towards the wooden wharf of the dock. His orders were carried out by the crew with precision.

"Lower the main sail, tighten that line," came the captain's gruff voice. The ship had been slowed as they had approached the dock. One sailor stood on the port side with a thick coil of mooring rope slung over his shoulder. As the ship came close to the wharf, the sailor jumped to the wooden planks and secured the rope to a thick wooden post.

"Drop the anchor," bellowed Captain Renshaw. "Bring us to a stop."

The ship lurched to a stop as the mooring rope snapped tight, the other two ships slowly glided in towards the dock. Derrel could hear the captains of the other ships calling out orders to bring them to a stop. Derrel walked over to where Captain Renshaw stood at the ship's wheel and surveyed the surrounding. No one had come to greet them, yet the dock had been built to receive ships and boats. The wooden wharfs led up on to the docks, where the posts had been sunk into the white sandy beaches. The sands of the beach stretched for a few hundred yards before ending in a thick screen of trees the like of which Derrel or Captain Renshaw had never seen before.

"Well, Sergeant," said the captain, "we made it and in one piece."

"Indeed, we did," replied Derrel. "I would like to thank you for a job well done, Captain. Would you please oversee the unloading of the cargo while my men and I seek out Lady Shamari?"

The captain was about to answer when a strange screeching sound came from the trees.

Tal's voice called out from the crow's nest. "Something's coming, Derrel," yelled the youth. "And it's coming fast."

"Can you see what it is?" shouted Derrel.

"No," replied Tal over the shrieking. "But whatever it is, there's a lot of them."

Derrel drew his arming sword from the scabbard on his back, leaving the sabre sheathed at his right hip.

"Defensive line," shouted the sergeant.

Instantly, the fifteen soldiers drew their weapons.

Captain Renshaw's gruff voice bellowed out. "Ready yourselves, my lads." The crew of the ship armed themselves with sabre's axes and stout wooden kludges. Tal had climbed down from the crow's nest and came to stand beside his brother.

"What the hell do you think you're doing?" snapped Derrel.

"Give me a sword, I can fight."

"No," stormed his brother. "Get back in that crow's nest or retreat to my cabin at once."

Anger showed on Tal's face. "What's the point of teaching me to fight if you won't let me defend myself?" stormed the youth. "For the past few months, I've done everything you said."

Derrel looked at his brother and drew his sabre, passing it to the youth. "Stay by my side," said Derrel. "Do not do anything stupid." Tal took the sabre and smiled.

The shrieking grew louder and louder, the look on the men's faces showed no fear as the trees started to move. From the tree line came one of the strangest sights Derrel had ever seen.

Around fifty giant birds burst through the foliage, their heads were like that of a giant eagle, their massive beaks hooked and yellow. The birds ran on towards the dock, their giant powerful legs throwing up the sprays of sand as they charged forward, but the strangest thing about the scene was the fact that a dwarf sat on the back of the giant bird, riding it like a horse.

The dwarves reined in the giant birds, some fifty feet away from the ship. One rider nudged his mount forward and pointed a spear towards Derrel. He spoke in a language the sergeant had never heard.

Corporal Didier leaned in and whispered in Derrel's ear, "Look at the spear, the blade is made from gold."

The giant bird shifted around, its head twitching from side to side. The lead dwarf removed his foot from the stirrup and slid from the back of the bird. Derrel noted the dwarf's attire; his arms were bare except for thick leather wrist guards that ended just before the elbow. He also wore a leather vest adorned with a silver shining vest of chain mail, his legs were bare and around his waist he wore a leather kilt studded with silver. On his feet, he wore black ankle-length boots topped with the brown feathers of the giant bird. The most noticeable difference Derrel saw was that the dwarf's dark hair and beard were closely cropped and their skin was also a dark brown, almost black. All of them had their hair and beards closely cropped.

Again, the dwarf repeated what he had said. When no answer came, the dwarf turned to his men, held the spear above his head and started to shout. the mounted dwarves all shouted back in unison, pointing their spears towards the ship. The lead dwarf spun on his heel and launched his spear at the docked ship. Derrel's sword flashed up, deflecting the spear slicing through the wooden shaft.

For a few moments, no one moved, then the dwarf who had dismounted drew a long, slim, silver-bladed axe from his saddle. The haft of the axe was four feet long with two thin sickle blades that were six inches wide and two and a half feet long. At least twelve inches of the blade ran up past the top of the haft, which made the axe look like a two-bladed spear. The dwarf pointed to Derrel once more and dragged the blade of his sickle axe across the wooden boards of the dock.

"I think he's challenging you," said Tal.

"Lower the gangplank," ordered Derrel.

"Wait," said Tal, dragging on his brother's jerkin. "What happened to don't do anything stupid?"

Derrel smiled at his brother. "Don't worry, this won't take long."

The gang plank clattered to the dock. Derrel started the walk towards the waiting dwarf warrior who stood with a malevolent smile on his face. Derrel started to twirl his sword in his hand, loosening the muscles and whispered a prayer to the God of Battle.

"Ristus, I offer you this death, guide my sword and accept the life I offer you."

As Derrel neared the dwarf, the warrior screamed his battle cry and ran forward, the sickle axe slashing at Derrel. His arming sword came up, deflecting the axe. The impact of the axe upon the sword was immense; Derrel felt the vibrations run down his arm, causing him to nearly lose his grip on the sword. The attack was fast and ferocious; the dwarf's attack was relentless.

The dwarf swung his sickle axe over his head, Derrel twisted to his right and the axe slammed into the wood of the dock, splintering one of the boards. Derrel slammed the guard of his sword to the side of the dwarf's head, causing the dwarf to stagger back. Derrel stepped forward, slashing his sword for his opponent's neck. The axe came up, deflecting Derrel's blade. With a flick of his wrist, Derrel's sword sliced across the back of his opponent's hand, cutting in deep. The dwarf released the axe; it clattered to the dock floor. The dwarf's eyes went wide as Derrel stepped in and smashed a left cross to the unprotected face of the dwarf, causing him to fall onto his back. Derrel stepped forward and placed the point of his sword to the neck of his opponent.

A golden spear slammed into the wooden boards next to Derrel's foot. The young sergeant jumped back, ready for another attack. Four more dwarfs had dismounted and were advancing on him. A sound like thunder erupted, followed by a bright flash of light that flashed between Derrel and the four advancing dwarfs. Derrel tried to shield his eyes from the light and staggered back as an unseen force hit him in the chest, pushing him away from the fallen dwarf. As his vision started to clear, there on the dock between the dwarfs and him stood a woman in blue robes. She wore her long black raven hair pulled back into a ponytail, which revealed her beautiful face. Her emerald green eyes flared with anger.

"Enough of this," stormed the woman.

The giant birds were barely being kept under control by their riders, their shrill squawks echoed through the air.

Derrel sheathed his sword and approached the blue-robed woman. Bowing deeply, he introduced himself. "Lady Shamari, I take it. I am Sergeant Derrel Mendez of His Royal Highness King Tyrin Degarre's army. His Highness sends his warmest and most profound greetings."

Lady Shamari was helping the dwarf Derrel had hit get back to his feet, she turned and fixed the young sergeant with an icy stare.

"You have been sent here on request of your king to open trade between your two nations and the first thing you do is start a fight with the chief's son?" snapped Shamari.

"My lady," said Derrel in a stern voice, "we were only defending ourselves; it was the dwarves who attacked us first."

Shamari turned back to the dwarf and spoke in their strange language. As the dwarf started to answer her, he couldn't meet her gaze. Shamari's voice grew sterner as she continued to talk to the dwarf. It seemed to Derrel that Shamari had some authority amongst the dwarves.

Turning back to Derrel, Shamari's mood seemed to have changed. "It seems you are correct," she said. "This is Darumi, he is the chief's son and he thought you and your men were raiders. When you did not answer him, he took your silence as a challenge."

"My lady, please inform him I did not answer as I did not understand his words."

Shamari was about to relay what Derrel had said but paused and smiled.

"I have a better way," she said.

Shamari started to move her fingers and hands, muttering words Derrel could never comprehend. Slowly, a white mist started to flow from her hands and surrounded Derrel's head. The mist flowed on towards the three ships and encircled the head of every crew member, then disappeared as quick as it had come. Shamari gestured to Derrel.

"Please tell Darumi what you have for him."

Derrel laughed. "He won't understand me, my good lady," he said.

"I understand you, human," said Darumi.

Derrel's eyes went wide with surprise. "How did you do that?" exclaimed the sergeant.

"I am capable of many a great things," said Shamari. "And I do not have time to play translator for you and your men. I have given you all the ability to understand the dwarves of this land."

"But how can they understand me?" interrupted Derrel. "I don't speak dwarven."

"You do now," said Shamari, smiling.

"Lady Shamari said you have something for us?" asked Darumi, his eyes scanning the ships.

Derrel regained his composure. "My king, His Royal Highness King Tyrin, has sent me here to open trade between our two peoples. He has sent steel for you," said Derrel, gesturing to the three ships behind him. "Each ship carries steel for your forges."

Darumi stepped forward and tapped a bloody finger to Derrel's chest plate. "Good steel," he said. "Will you also offer this as a gift?"

"Sadly, no," said Derrel. "This is armour of the royal army; it is a punishable offence for a soldier not to have his armour."

Darumi smiled. "We will give you gold for the steel," he said. "Come, I will take you to see my father. He will be eager to meet you." Darumi walked to his mount and removed a length of cloth to bind the cut on his hand. The bird squatted, allowing the dwarf to get into the strange saddle. "I will leave thirty of my men to help with the steel, Lady Shamari will show you the way."

Without another word, he turned his mount and rode off, shouting his orders to his men.

Chapter Thirteen

The wedding had gone ahead one week after Tyrin had announced his betrothal to Emelia. Most of the dukes and barons had attended the royal wedding, but all had showed their displeasure in the choice of Tyrin's bride. The whole of Carthage had been involved in the celebration, the king had ordered food and drink to be sent to every home within the city. Even some of the city's populace had been let into the palace to enjoy the festivities. The palace had been decorated with huge white and gold banners that had been hung from the palace walls and from the internal balconies. All the soldiers were dressed in their finest armour, the king himself had worn the armour from the battle with Sagoth. This had been cleaned and polished to a shine.

The Duke of Movale had brought his two daughters and his wife to watch the king and Emelia wed. Much to the dismay of his two daughters, their father had been drinking to excess and had been overheard by General Kaylin talking to the duke of Wroving.

"I'll tell you this much, my dear fellow," Cedric had belched, "my eldest daughter Adelphia would have made a fantastic queen and wife for His Highness. Just take a look at her," said the duke, pointing with a flabby hand to where his family were sat. "Heartbroken she is," slurred the duke. "It should be my daughter the king is marrying, I have the largest duchy after Carthage."

"I agree," responded the Duke of Wroving drunkenly, trying to focus his eyes on where Cedric was pointing. "Your daughters are beautiful, they both have fine childbearing hips."

Kaylin glanced over at the duke's family, both of his daughters shared their father's elaborate taste in colourful clothing, and both of them shared their father's figure, which was emphasised by their colourful gowns.

"Gods help us," said Kaylin, smiling and stifling a laugh; only in their father's eye were these women beautiful.

Tyrin had made a speech later that night, thanking all in attendance for sharing in his joyous day. The new queen, Emelia, had looked divine in a white silk gown laced with silver thread, she had been the envy of every woman in attendance and how they had shown their discontent at the most powerful man in the kingdom marrying a commoner.

Summer had turned to autumn, bringing a chill to the air. Now Tyrin faced new problems; he had held council and his advisers had warned of a harsh winter to come and that food stock would run dangerously low. Snow had settled on the palace grounds white and crisp, huge icicles hung down like swords from the battlements.

General Kaylin sat in his private rooms nursing a goblet of red wine, a fire had been lit in the ornate fire place, casting dancing shadows around the room. He had not heard anything from his son now for near on six months, the last raven had arrived one month after the ship had departed on her voyage, informing the general all was going well and that Derrel had started training Tal in combat to keep him out of trouble. A light tapping came at the general's door.

"Enter," called out Kaylin.

The door opened and Tyrin entered the room. Kaylin made to stand.

"No, my friend," said Tyrin. "Please remain seated, you look tired."

Kaylin smiled. "I am, Your Majesty," he said. "It would be nice to hear if Derrel and the ships have made it safely to Rainoa."

Tyrin produced a small scroll bearing his seal from his blue tunic. "A request to High Castle," said Tyrin. "I have asked for Elazar to attend and try and commune with Lady Shamari, I too hunger for news."

"How is the queen?" asked Kaylin.

Tyrin smiled once more. "Emelia is tired, the pregnancy is going well. The midwife says that she has only three months until the child is born."

"Is it wise to request Elazar?" asked Kaylin. "Knowing his feelings towards this."

"A pox on Elazar," sneered Tyrin. "We were able to beat Sagoth once so why would he not fall a second time? Besides, I have sent the gem piece where no one will find it, and when you and I are gone, my friend, there will be no living person on this world who will know its whereabouts."

Kaylin poured wine into a second goblet and offered it to Tyrin who accepted it gratefully. "Do you still intend to take the trip to the Great Forest once your child is born?" asked Kaylin.

Tyrin raised the goblet and took a long drink. "I will wait till the spring and all the snows have melted," said Tyrin. "This is the first time that humans have been invited to visit the land of the elves. King Alinar has agreed to trade between our kingdoms."

"I will be accompanying you," said Kaylin in a tone that did not leave any room for argument.

Tyrin gave a little chuckle. "I did not doubt it, my friend, and

I would not be without my champion." Tyrin drained the goblet. "Well, it's late, my friend, and the queen will be asleep by now. You should get some rest," he told Kaylin. "Tomorrow, Elazar should be here and we will learn of our mission across the sea." Placing the goblet on a table, Tyrin bid the general a good night.

Kadius had journeyed through the Black Mountains for what seemed an eternity, the landscape was harsh and bleak. Here and there, he had seen the odd lone goblin watching him, its green-brown skin the only flash of colour in this dark desolate place. It would be there one second and then it would scurry away to hide. It felt to Kadius that he was being watched from all angles.

A chilly wind blew down from the north, Kadius shivered and pulled his arms to his chest. Instantly, thick black fur-lined robes covered his body, and a heavy hood covered his head.

"You can now see what power lies within one piece of the gem," came Sagoth's voice in his head. *"Think of what you will be able to accomplish when we have all four pieces."*

Kadius trudged on in silence through the snow, his thoughts were of his life back in High Castle. For forty years, he had studied the mystical arts, and he had gained the mantel of master mage at the age of twenty, becoming the youngest mage to be given that title. He had hoped that his powers would give him the longevity like the other three masters, but this was not to be. He had watched his body age and his hair slowly recede and turn grey. He had truly believed that after touching the gem piece that his powers had been truly awakened and that he could become more powerful than Elazar.

A spear slammed into the rock near his head, sparks flashed as the spear bounced away. Kadius froze. In front of him stood a tall orc warrior dressed in a white bear skin robe.

"You are far from home, human," said the orc. "You look young and strong, you will make good meat to feed our army."

Shrill laughter came from all directions, followed by the sound of falling rock, and the sound of steel scraping on stone followed as orcs clambered out from their hiding places. From all directions, orcs came scrambling into view.

Kadius took a step backwards as an orc warrior levelled a spear and hurled it straight at him. Instinctively, Kadius raised his arms in a vain attempt to block the spear.

The spear bounced from Kadius and clattered to the floor; the laughter of the orcs ceased. Xruul stepped forward, wrenched a spear from another orcs hand and hurled it with all his might at the darkly garbed human. Once more, the spear bounced harmlessly away.

"Kill him!" roared Xruul.

Spears and axes were hurled at Kadius. Orcs ran in to hack at him with swords; all were repelled by an unseen force. The orc warriors began to look at one another then at Xruul, not one blade had touched the mysterious dark-robed human.

The voice that came from Kadius was not his; it was deeper, and the tone was commanding.

"Return to Urag and tell him his master summons him at the Dark Fortress, there is work to be done."

Without anther word, the dark-robed figure turned and walked away from the stunned orcs.

Chapter Fourteen

The thirty dwarfs had dismounted from their mounts and had started to help unload the three ships. The giant birds had gathered on the white sand and were squatted down, dozing in the early afternoon sun. Derrel had taken Lady Shamari to his cabin where she was briefing him on the customs of the dwarves of Rainoa.

Tal had taken to wandering round the docks. The thirteen-year-old had removed his boots and had rolled his grey leggings up to his knees. The waters of the dock were as clear as glass, not at all like the waters of home that had a murky green colour to them. Tal watched in fascination as small silver fish darted in and out of the shallows. He still had the sabre that his brother had given him. Slowly, he waded out until the water touched his leggings, then he stopped and stood statue-still with the sabre raised above his head in a reversed grip. Here, larger fish were swimming, there silver scales shining like precious metal. The youngster stood stock still, waiting for a fish to swim closer.

Tal readied himself to strike. "One fat silver fish coming up," he whispered.

"What the hell are you doing?" shouted Derrel as Tal's arm dropped. The youth looked up at the sound of his brother's voice, causing him to lose his footing and plunge face-first under the water.

Tal came up coughing and spluttering to the laughter of the sailors and dwarves. The youth looked at the end of his sabre; he had missed the fish.

"Thanks, Derrel," said the youth in a disapproving tone. "You just cost me my dinner."

"There's food on the ship," said Derrel as Tal made his way up the beach.

"I know that," replied Tal. "But I wanted a nice fresh fish for my dinner."

The youth was removing his wet jerkin as he walked, he had been looking at his brother the whole time. "You could have waited until I had skewered that fish before distracting me." Derrel lifted his arm and pointed. "What now?" asked Tal, turning and coming face to face with one of the giant birds.

Tal froze as the bird lent its head forward, its large tawny eye blinking. The bird's head moved from side to side. Slowly, Tal started to back away. Suddenly, the bird squawked and snapped at the youth, its razor-sharp beak plucking the wet jerking from Tal's hand which caused him to lose his footing once more. Tal landed on the soft sand.

"Be careful around the war birds," said Shamari. "If they don't know your scent, they will try and bite you."

Tal stood and brushed the sand form him the best he could as he made his way back onto the dock.

"Do you know something?" he said to his brother as he walked past him. "I actually miss being at sea." The youth headed up the gang plank and onto the ship, still grumbling.

"We should make our way to see the dwarf chief," said Shamari. "Darumi will have reached home by now and will have told the chief of your arrival."

"You mentioned raiders earlier. Who are they and where do they come from?"

"To the south, there are a small cluster of islands. The

dwarves call them Sea Dogs. From time to time, the Sea Dogs will chance a landing and try and raid the dwarf settlements. They are human, but spend most of their life at sea, their skin is darkened like that of the Chambia Nomads but not as dark as the dwarves' skin. They too prize steel above all other metals, but they have been known to take the dwarven woman as well."

Derrel's eyes widened, the look on his face showed he understood why they took the women.

"Yes, Sergeant," said Shamari.

"Is there anything else I should know of?" asked Derrel.

"Yes," replied the mage. "The main threat on this land comes from the drows."

Derrel raised an eyebrow. "Drows?"

"A race of elves," Shamari continued. "The dwarves refer to them as the dark elves. They look pretty much like the elves of Sharr, but the main difference is these elves are more feral. All the drows have dark hair and violet eyes, their faces look like they have pale white skin, but the skin has soft fine white fur upon it."

"Are we likely to encounter these drows?"

"It is hard to say, but if you do, be ready to kill them before they kill you."

Corporal Didier approached. "The first ship has been unloaded, sir," he reported.

"Good," answered Derrel. "I will be accompanying Lady Shamari, I will leave you to supervise the rest of the unloading, Corporal, and please keep an eye on my young brother while I'm gone."

"Yes, sir," replied Didier, saluting. "Will you be taking the king's gift for the dwarf chief with you, sir?" the corporal asked.

"No," Derrel replied. "I will give that to the chief as a parting gift," Didier saluted. "Shall we?" asked Derrel, pointing in the direction that Darumi had gone.

Shamari had taken the lead as they set off, with Derrel a few paces behind. The sun was obscured by the thick vegetation of the trees, but the humidity of this land was making Derrel uncomfortable. Derrel noted the leaves of the trees. He had never seen their like; one leaf was as long as a tall man and as wide as Derrel at the hips and then plunged to a point. They had been walking for thirty minutes when a strange chattering sound came from the trees. Derrel's arming sword flashed out of its scabbard.

"Get behind me, my lady," shouted Derrel, his eyes darting from side to side.

Shamari let out a soft sweet chuckle and placed her hand on Derrel's, lowering the sword. "It's all right, Sergeant," she said, pointing up to the treetops.

Derrel looked up to see flashes of black and white fur as small creatures leaped from tree to tree, chattering as they went by. "What are they?" he asked.

"The dwarves call them monkeys," answered Shamari. "They are quite harmless."

"What other creatures live in this forest?" asked Derrel.

"This is no forest, Sergeant; this is a jungle and there are creatures that live in here that are very dangerous."

"I have never met anyone or anything that I couldn't kill with my sword."

Shamari looked at the young officer. "Well, let's hope we make it without having to put that to the test," she said.

For over an hour, they walked through the thick vegetation of the jungle. Derrel could see the tracks left by the war birds. Long strides had been left between the footprints. He paced out the distance.

"What are you doing?" asked Shamari.

"Those war birds can cover over four metres in a single stride," said Derrel. "How fast can they run?"

"In comparison to what?" asked Shamari.

"Compare it to a horse," said Derrel.

"I would say that the birds could run twice as fast as a horse, but the horse could cover more distance; the stamina of the birds is not as great as that of a horse."

The two companions continued to walk. Shamari noticed Derrel's hand go for his sword another seven times when a different animal of the jungle called out. Finally, Derrel heard a sound that he recognised; the sound of people. The thick vegetation of the jungle came to an abrupt stop.

Derrel looked down upon a vast city that shone like gold, the city had been carved out into a huge valley. Its golden buildings stretching as far as the eye could see. The city was easily bigger than Carthage, with a huge mountain range on its horizon.

"Sergeant Mendez, welcome to the golden city of Udila," said Shamari, sweeping out her arm. "Let's go find the chief, he will be eager to meet you."

Derrel looked on in amazement, the entire city gleamed like gold in the sunlight.

Derrel walked beside Shamari. Everywhere he looked, there seemed to be a throng of people. All of them seemed to be busy doing something or going somewhere. As Derrel got further into the city, he noticed that the temperature was getting warmer. Derrel reached up and wiped his forehead with the sleeve of his jerking. Once again, he noticed that all the male inhabitants had on leather kilts that were cut into strips, studded with gold or silver. The jerkings the men wore were sleeveless and high cut onto the shoulder. He also noticed that the dwarf women wore thin cotton dresses that were worn high on the thigh. These too were worn very high cut onto the shoulders and the front of the dress plunged down, exposing the woman's cleavage and their smooth dark skin.

"Do you see something you like?" asked Shamari, smiling.

Derrel flushed a little. "Do all the women here wear such little clothing?"

"If they wore a heavier garment, they would surly pass out with the heat," she replied.

Derrel looked at her. "But you are wearing that heavy blue robe, my lady. How is it that the heat is not affecting you?"

With a wave of her hand, Shamari whispered a word of power. Instantly, Derrel felt as if a cool breeze was gently blowing at him.

"I did tell you I was capable of many a great thing."

"Magic?" said Derrel.

"Now that you are more comfortable, shall we press onto the chief's lodge? He will be expecting us."

Derrel followed Lady Shamari on through winding streets, past shops, taverns and market stalls. Everywhere they went, it became apparent to Derrel that gold was plentiful here. The hinges and handles of the doors were made from gold, statues in the street had been cast from the precious metal. If someone were to collect the gold from just one street, they would be as rich as a duke. A person could afford to buy an estate in Sharr and have servants to tend to them for the rest of their lives.

"Where does all the gold come from?" asked Derrel.

Shamari pointed to the mountains in the distance. "The dwarves have been mining those mountains for hundreds of years. A few centuries ago, they discovered steel in the mountains. The dwarves made tools and weapons from the steel which turn the tide in battle with the drows. Now the drows attack the steel mines using the ogres."

"Ogres!" exclaimed Derrel. "I have heard of them, but I've never seen one. Are they as big as the stories say?"

"They are," said Shamari, "and very difficult to kill. Their skin is extremely thick. I have heard stories form the chief that warriors have bent golden blades trying to stab an ogre, that's why the dwarves want steel."

After a few hours of walking, Derrel and Shamari came to what Derrel thought must be the chief's home. The building was dome-shaped and huge in comparison to the other dwellings. It was not as grand as Tyrin's palace, but the amount of gold that had been used to construct the building was ridiculous. Huge columns of gold had been erected on the two-storey building; gold ornate hinges held the thick pale wooden doors in place. The walls that surrounded the chief's lodge were ten feet high, topped with golden railings. Inside the grounds of the chief's lodge, dwarves tended to the gardens, trimming bushes and trees and tending to the brightly coloured flowerbeds. All worked with golden gardening tools. As Derrel and Shamari approached the lodge, the large wooden doors swung open and Derrel recognised the face of Darumi as he came walking out. Behind him came a dwarf dressed in a white leather kilt and a short-sleeved white jerkin. His steel-grey hair and beard were closely cropped like all the other dwarf males, but looked strange in contrast to his dark skin. He still looked powerful like all the dwarf males did despite his large belly.

Derrel whispered to Shamari, "I take it this is the chief?"

"Indeed, it is," she said, bowing. "Greetings, Chief Detas," she said aloud. "May I present to you Sergeant Derrel Mendez from the royal army of King Tyrin."

The chief stepped forward and kissed the hand of Shamari, then he shook Derrel's hand. His grip was strong and firm.

"Welcome, my boy." His voice sounded like rumbling thunder. "I hope you have brought plenty of steel for me and my men."

"Indeed, I have, Chief Detas," replied Derrel. "My men are unloading the ships as we speak."

"Excellent," said the chief, his voice was exuberant. He turned to his son. "Darumi, take a detachment of men and wagons, I want you to personally see that the steel is brought here safely. And this time, don't pick a fight with our new friends," said Detas, smiling.

Darumi bowed. "Yes, Father, at once." Darumi turned and ran to the side of his father's lodge, calling for his men.

"You must be hungry," said Detas. "Please," he said, gesturing to the open doors. "Allow me to offer you refreshments."

Shamari bowed. "If you will excuse me," she said to the two men, "I must return to the construction of the gateway."

"Of course," said Detas. "Will you join us for the evening meal, my lady?"

"I will, indeed," she replied, smiling at Derrel. She turned and walked away. Derrel felt a strange sense fall upon him as the mysterious woman left.

"Come along then, Sergeant, let us talk of your king's terms and the future between our two nations." Detas looked at Derrel who had started to sweat again. "And maybe we can find you something more comfortable to wear."

Chapter Fifteen

Tal had changed his clothes, hanging the wet garments on the ship's rail. He had looked 'round, trying to find his brother, but he was nowhere to be seen. He decided to climb back up to the crow's nest. Tal had watched as the sailors and the dwarves started unloading the creates of steel and stack them on the dock.

Something caused the sleeping war birds to stir from their lazy doze in the sun. The birds on the beach started to squawk. In the distance, Tal could hear what had stirred them; more of the birds were approaching through the trees. The ones on the beach were answering the call of the ones approaching through the jungle.

The sound grew louder as Tal watched with fascination. Suddenly, war birds burst through the trees. Tal noticed that some of them had been hitched to wagons. He shivered, their shrill calls unnerved the youth.

He had come face to face with one. Even squatted down, the birds were as tall as Tal. When they were stood up, the birds were above ten feet tall. The dwarves ran to the gathered birds to quieten them down. Thirty wagons in total had been brought by the dwarves, all of them containing wooden crates.

Corporal Didier approached the lead wagon and removed a hunting knife from his belt. Placing the knife blade under the lid, he pried one of the creates open. Bars of gold glistened in the sunlight. Didier pressed the lid back into place.

"Start the loading," commanded the corporal.

Tal settled down in the crow's nest and soon drifted off to sleep.

Shouts from below awoke him. The sun had started to set, turning the sky a deep orange. He heard the familiar sound of swords clashing and the shouts of injured men. Tal chanced a glance over the edge of the nest and saw that the dwarves and their war birds had gone. The soldiers and sailors had formed a defensive line on the dock. A few of the sailors lay dead on the ground with arrows jutting from their bodies, while the rest of men were fighting off tall dark-haired warriors dressed in dark green clothing. Corporal Didier was calling out orders to the men while Captain Renshaw was vainly trying to loosen the mooring rope. More and more of the tall dark-haired warriors came from the trees, losing shafts into the defending men. Captain Renshaw took an arrow high in the chest and fell from the dock.

Tal wanted to call out to him, but knew it would be futile to do so. More and more of the men went down as the tall warriors loosed shaft after shaft onto the men below. The last man to fall was Corporal Didier; he died as an arrow pierced his skull right between the eyes. Only a couple of the tall dark-haired warriors had fallen. These had died as the king's soldiers had rushed forward to hack at them before falling to a volley of arrows. The tall warriors moved cautiously forward, bows bent.

A groan came from one of the fallen soldiers on the dock. One of the advancing warriors drew a golden blade, he knelt down and grabbed the wounded man by the hair and pulled him into a seated position. Coldly, he drew the blade across the man's throat, spilling out his life's blood. The soldier died without making another sound. When the warriors had finished searching all the bodies, they boarded the ships and started the search.

Tal didn't move a muscle as he watched the warriors strip

the ship bare, stacking the metal they had plundered from them. When they had finished with the ship, they moved onto the dead soldiers, stripping them of armour and weapons. One of the warriors came from Derrel's cabin, carrying the ornate wooden box. The tall warrior shouted something to someone Tal presumed was the leader. The warrior with the box opened the lid and the leader removed the golden hammer. He swung the hammer as if testing the weight, then passed it back to the warrior with the box.

The leader pulled a horn from his belt and let out a long dulcet tone. From the treeline came a score of the biggest creatures Tal had ever seen; the creatures were easily twelve feet tall, their skin was a golden brown with thick black coarse hair on their fore arms and legs. They wore a simple loin cloth around their waste, but what Tal noted the most was the huge curled ram-like horns that grew from the sides of their heads. The horns of these creatures looked to be as smooth as glass and were shiny black. Large tusk-like teeth stuck up from the bottom lip of the creatures and the faces were the ugliest thing Tal had ever seen.

The large creatures dragged huge leather packs with them. The dark-haired warrior started to shout and point at the huge creatures. On his command, they opened the leather packs while the tall warriors started to load in the metal from the ships and from the dead soldiers. Tal watched as the box containing the hammer was placed in with the other stolen items. The large creatures hefted the leather packs to their back and ambled off back into the trees, followed by the tall warriors. Half a dozen of the warriors stayed behind, they took something from their belts then. Tall watched as they started to strike at the flint and set the arrows alight; he knew what would come next. The darkly garbed warriors loosed the flaming arrows at the ships. Flames started to catch along the ships, and the remaining warriors turned and followed after the others into the trees.

As soon as the last of them disappeared, Tal scrambled from his hiding place. Quickly, he started his descent and managed to get to the yard mast but could go no further. The ships were fully ablaze now, and the flames were climbing the masts. The heat was intense as the seasoned timbers burnt. Thick black smoke was making it hard to breath. Gingerly, Tal made his way along the yard mast. The flames had reached the sails which instantly caught alight. Flames shot along the dry ropes and the rigging of the ship. Tal had nowhere to go, he closed his eyes and leapt from the yard mast to the waiting waters below.

The air burst from Tal's lungs as he hit the water. Frantically, he swam for the surface, taking in a great gulp of air as he broke through the surface. Tal swam away from the burning ships; the fire had now spread to the wooden dock. Large plumes of smoke were drifting skyward as the seasoned timbers cracked and popped under the heat of the flames. He managed to get to the beach. The youth stood and watched as the ships burnt to nothing. Despair hit him; he was alone, everyone was dead and his brother was somewhere out there, but Tal had no idea which way to go.

Chapter Sixteen

The sky had started to darken. The remains of the ships burnt in contrast with the setting sun. Tal walked back towards where the dock had stood, the smell of burning flesh drifted on the evening breeze. From time to time, there was the sound of popping coming from the burning wood, as cinders lifted from the remains of the fire to drift away on the breeze. Tal surmised that if he had survived, then there could be a chance that someone else had too. If he called out, would the tall dark-haired warriors hear him? Tal drew his sabre and took a deep breath.

"Is anyone still alive?" he called. No answer came. "Please," called the youth again. "Is anyone there?" One of the burning timbers popped loudly to Tal's left. The youth spun, sabre raised in defence.

Something moved on the beach around twenty paces from him. Someone was crawling up the beach out of the water. Tal slammed his sabre back in its scabbard and ran towards the man. As he approached, he saw that Captain Renshaw had survived the fall and the blaze. Tal felt a sense of relief as he dropped to his knees on the sand and turned over the captain to lay on his back, the arrow which had struck him in the chest had snapped off, leaving a couple of inches sticking out. The left side of the captain's face and body had been burnt badly. His clothes had burned and were now stuck to his burnt and blackened skin.

"Captain," said Tal, looking at the injured man. "What can I do?"

Renshaw coughed and placed a hand on Tal's leg. "Did anyone else survive?" he asked weakly. Tal shook his head, tears had started to flow down his cheeks.

"No," whispered Tal, his voice breaking. "Just you and I are all that are left."

"Listen, boy," said Renshaw. "You must find your brother."

"How?" asked Tal. "I don't know which way he went."

Renshaw weakly grabbed hold of Tal's jerkin. "Listen to me, boy," he said. "Go up the beach, you will find an outcrop of rocks. Turn right, walk about forty paces towards the trees and you will see a small cave. I found it while the men were unloading the ships. Take shelter there for the night. In the morning, head into the trees and go find your brother and that woman he went with."

"No," cried Tal. "I can't."

"You must, lad, those men could come back. If they find you here, they'll kill you."

"What about you?" asked Tal.

Renshaw shook his head. "I'm done for, lad," he said. With a shaky hand, the captain pulled a hunting knife from his belt. "Take it," he whispered weakly. Tal took the knife. As he did, the captain's arm dropped to the sand, his eyes staring vacantly up at the sky.

Removing his jerking and placing it over the captain's face, Tal stood, a huge shuddering breath left his body. He had liked the captain, he had treated the youngster like a grown up. Something moved behind him; pain erupted in his head. The blow from the sword hilt sent Tal face-first into the sand. Strong hands took hold of Tal's leg and he felt himself being pulled along the sand, then darkness came as he passed out.

Derrel had listened to the dwarf chief tell his stories of the battles with the drows, and the raids from the Sea Dogs, and how the dwarves had at one time traded with these men, but on the discovery of steel the Sea Dogs had started to raid the dwarven settlements, making them bitter enemies.

Derrel came to the conclusion that the chief liked the sound of his own voice. He told Derrel that the Drows had enslaved the ogres, using the large mindless creatures to attack the dwarves.

"You see, Sergeant," continued Detas, "the drows are extremely good archers and can shoot the wings off a mosquito from two hundred paces, but in hand-to-hand combat, they are not a match for the strength of my warriors. But ogres, those things are hard to kill. It was my grandfather that had first used the war birds to attack the ogres. He trained them as war mounts. A warbird's beak can sever the arm clean off an ogre," said Detas. "But the only problem is that if an ogre latches onto you, he or she will crush you. They are terribly strong. I once saw an ogre rip the arms clean off one of my warriors," laughed Detas.

"Tell me, Sergeant, have you ever faced an ogre?"

"No, my lord," replied Derrel. "I have fought a troll before; they sound similar except for the difference in height. Orcs tend to use them in much the same way as the drows use the ogres. A troll is not the most intelligent creature, but they are strong. We usually shoot them full of arrows from a distance to weaken them. It's the orcs that are the real problem. We scattered the orc armies in the last battle, they fled back into the Black Mountains of the north. Dunan and his dwarf warriors played a big part in our victory," admitted Derrel.

"I would very much like to meet this Dunan," said Detas. "He sounds like a great fellow."

The sound of horns came from outside of the chief's lodge. Detas smiled. "It seems that my son has returned. Come, let's go see what your king has sent me."

Derrel breathed a sigh of relief. He was eager to see Lady Shamari again and be free of the barrage of questions the chief had thrown at him.

"Come, my new friend," said the chief, leading the way out of the lodge.

The thirty wagons had been drawn up in the grounds of the chief's home, the war birds squawked and snapped at the air as Derrel and Detas came walking from the lodge.

"Look, Father," said Darumi, opening one of the creates and pulling out a steel ingot the size of his fist. He tossed it to his father. The chief examined the steel.

"This is high quality," said Detas. "How much more will King Tyrin send; I will match the weight of steel with that of gold."

"I'm afraid that my king's answer will take quite some time, Chief Detas," said Derrel. "For me and my men to return to Sharr will take six months at sea."

"I may be able to help with that," came the voice of Shamari.

Derrel turned, his breath catching in his throat. Shamari approached the group of dwarves. She was wearing a white dress like that of the dwarven women, her long dark hair hung loose down her shoulders. Her smooth skin shone like ivory in the light of the three moons.

"My lady," said Derrel, bowing. "I know you have the ability to commune with the other mages back on Sharr, but as I was just saying, it would be another year before I could return with another load of steel."

Shamari bowed to the chief. "With your permission, I will take the sergeant here and show him what I and your builders have been doing for the past year."

"As you wish, my lady," said Detas. "My men and I will take the steel to the forges."

Shamari bowed to the chief then took Derrel by the hand and led him away.

"Thank you for rescuing me," said Derrel. "The chief is an agreeable person, but he does like the sound of his own voice."

Shamari chuckled. "Yes, he does," she agreed. "Once he kept me up all night talking about his people's history."

"You said you would be able to aid me with the king's decision on the transport of more steel to the dwarves," said Derrel. "How, has his highness already sent another ship?"

"No," replied Shamari. "I was sent here over a year ago when Tyrin and Elazar first heard of this land, both the king and Elazar knew of the distance involved and the risk of such a long voyage. We had to come up with a way to be able to move between the two places without the need of ships."

"I'm afraid that would be impossible—" began Derrel.

Shamari placed her right index finger to his lips. "The mages of Sharr have the ability to move themselves over great distances. For instance, I could transport myself from here to the dock where we first met in the blink of an eye, but it takes a lot of magic to do that. the greater the spell the more magic a mage uses," she spoke.

"Could you transport yourself back to Sharr?" asked Derrel.

Shamari shook her head. "No, the distance is too far even for Elazar and he is the most powerful mage in the kingdoms."

"Then how?" asked Derrel.

"Let me show you," said Shamari. She led Derrel from the chief's grounds and on through the streets until they came to an area of what looked like warehouses. Shamari led Derrel towards a pair of huge wooden doors.

"Open them," she said.

Derrel pulled on one of the doors, swinging it open. Inside the warehouse, it was as dark as night. Shamari whispered a word of power. Slowly, a small glowing ball formed on her right hand and drifted into the darkness, illuminating the warehouse. In the centre stood two large white stone pillars that were twenty feet high and spaced twenty feet apart. A third huge pillar lay horizontal, spanning the top of the two pillars, creating a massive doorway. Gold runes had been inlayed into the stone pillars that wrapped all the way around the six-foot wide stones. As the runes reached the floor, Derrel noticed that the pillars had been set into a white stone circle that had been polished to a smooth finish. The golden runes extended into the floor and continued all the way to the edge of the stone circle.

"What is it?" asked Derrel, looking at the structure in awe.

"This is how we will move the shipments of gold and steel," said Shamari. "There is another of these being built in Carthage at the rear of the palace. When it is finished and I have imbued it with power, a gateway will be opened up between the two points, allowing us to pass from Rainoa to Carthage in the blink of an eye."

Derrel walked to the pillars and ran his hand over the smooth stone. "This is truly amazing," he said. "There will be no need for the long voyage. Can you show me Carthage now?" he asked.

"No," answered Shamari. "I still need to imbue this gate with more magic. It will take me a few more months yet, but I would like to show you something else," she said.

Derrel turned. As he did, Shamari took hold of his hand and kissed him. Her lips were soft and tasted sweet. Derrel took a step back.

"My lady," he said, blushing.

Shamari reached up and let the simple cotton dress fall to the floor. Her pale skin looked smooth as marble in the light from the orb, her breasts were firm and round. Derrel drank in the beauty of the woman before him.

"Do you like what you see?" she asked.

"I do my lady" stammered Derrel,

"Good," she said, snapping her fingers. Instantly, the orb disappeared.

The door to the warehouse opened, letting the sunlight stream in. Derrel shielded his eyes from the light. He had fallen asleep alongside Lady Shamari after their love making, but Shamari was nowhere to be seen.

"There you are," said Darumi. "I have been looking for you."

"Is something wrong?" asked Derrel.

"You need to come with me," said Darumi. "Your ships have been attacked; one of our scouts came back this morning and has reported the attack."

Derrel got to his feet and started to dress. "Wait, Sergeant," said Darumi. "You will be far too hot in your clothes. I have brought these for you." Darumi tossed a leather kilt and vest to Derrel. "I have mounts waiting for us."

Chapter Seventeen

Tal's head throbbed. He was being carried, he knew that much. A small shaft of light came in through a small split in the leather sack he was being carried in. He had no idea how long he had been inside the sack. Tal kept sinking back into unconsciousness, all he knew was that he was thirsty and his head hurt.

Cold water woke the youth as it was splashed onto his face. A piece of cloth had been tied across his face, restricting his vision. Something touched his lips and he felt the coolness of the water flow into his mouth; the water was sweet. Tal drank greedily. Strong hands grabbed him by his wrists which were bound, and he was hauled to his feet. Tal looked down from under the cloth which restricted his vision, he could see the dark green leggings and the dark boots of his capturer.

There was a tug at the rope which bound his wrist, causing him to lurch forward. He was being led through the jungle at a steady pace. Tal had no idea how many of his captors there were; he heard at least three different voices that he could distinguish.

After what seemed an eternity, a halt was called. Strong hands pushed Tal to the ground and a water container was pushed to his lips. He took three long gulps before the water was taken away from him. He then felt something pushed into his hand; it was soft and moist. Lifting it to his nose, he smelt at it. The smell was sweet and made his mouth water. Quickly, he ate it. The taste was divine and sweet juices ran down his throat. Tal had been so focused on trying to see what was happening around him, he had forgotten all about his stomach; he was ravenous.

From under the cloth that bound his eyes, Tal saw the dark green boots in front of him. He watched as the wearer lifted his foot and placed it on Tal's chest. The booted foot pushed Tal to the ground, then he heard a strange language he did not understand. Tal tried to sit up, but felt the booted foot push him back down and the words were repeated. He lay still, and the boot was removed from his chest. Sleep finally came to the youth.

Tal was awoken once more by cold water touching his lips. After he had drunk once more, he was pulled to his feet and forced to walk blindfolded through the jungle. After what seemed an eternity, again he was pushed to the ground, fed and made to sleep. The next day, the same thing happened again and the day after. As night fell, Tal lay feigning sleep. He waited for the camp to go quiet and slipped the blindfold from his eyes, then expertly he slipped the bonds on his wrists and then lay still once more. After a few minutes, he quietly rose to his feet and peered around the camp.

No fires had been lit which held the camp in complete darkness. Tal could just make out the forms of the bodies sleeping on the ground of the dark clad warriors, and the huge hulking forms of the large beasts. Quietly, Tal snuck away, making no sound. He had no idea where he was going; he just knew he needed to get away. Tal crept on for fifty paces, judging this to be a far enough distance for him to run. A blow to the back of the head sent him face-first to the jungle floor.

Tal awoke; his head was pounding and his hands and feet had been bound. Slowly, he opened his eyes. Blurred figures moved around the youth. As his vision started to clear, he recognised the tall dark-haired warriors that had attacked the ships. Slowly, he reached for his sabre; it was missing. Tal was laid on a cold hard floor inside a stone building with a thatch roof. The young squire tried to look around without letting his captors know he was awake. Sunlight streamed in from a small window behind him.

Tal noticed the room was sparse of furniture, there was a table in front of him and a couple of chairs. The walls were a dull grey stone that made the room feel cold despite the heat from the sun. Hands grabbed a hold of Tal, dragging him to his feet.

Tal found himself looking into large violet eyes of one of the men. The features of his captors were strange; soft white fur covered their faces and arms, yet Tal found the face soft and strangely beautiful. The long dark hair had been pulled back to the nape of the neck into a ponytail. The creature in front of him spoke, the words seemed musical like the soft purring of a cat.

"I don't understand," said Tal.

"Dwarf, you speak dwarf?" said the creature. "You are no dwarf, you are human like the Sea Dogs."

"I don't know who the Sea Dogs are," said Tal, panicking.

"If you are not from the Sea Dogs, where are you from? Your ships had much steel on them; where did you get the steel from?" asked his captor.

"I'm from across the sea," said Tal. "From a land called Sharr. We have plenty of steel, our king sent us here to trade steel for gold."

"What is a king?"

"He is our leader," said Tal.

"You will take me and my men to this king and we will trade for steel."

"I can't take you," said Tal.

The drow struck him across the face with the back of his hand. "If you don't take me to this king, I will feed you to the ogres."

"If I could take you, I would, but you burnt our ships, and it would take us many months to cross the sea."

The drow raised his hand to strike Tal once more.

"Wait," cried the youth flinching. "We brought steel for the dwarves; they have lots of steel now."

The drow lowered his hand and dropped Tal back to the floor. He turned to the other four in the room and spoke in the strange purring language. After a quick conversation, he turned back to Tal.

"I am Tolomyn Tlin'arran of the elves. What is your name, human?"

"I am Tal Mendez of Sharr. I mean no harm to you," said the youth. The five drows in the room started to laugh. One of the drows walked to a table that was against a wall and picked up Tal's sabre and passed it to Tolomyn.

"You have a nice sword," said Tolomyn. "This is good steel," he said, drawing the blade. "Can you use it?"

Tal nodded his head. "My brother has been teaching me," he said. "He is the greatest swordsman in Sharr; no man can beat him." This made the drows in the room laugh once more.

"I would very much like to meet this brother and test what you say. You humans are slow and weak, this brother you speak of would die easy fighting an elf warrior."

"You are wrong," said Tal, anger flaring inside him giving him confidence. "My brother would carve his way through all five of you as easy as a fish glides through water." Tolomyn struck Tal in the face once more.

"Take him to the slave pens."

Two of the drows seized Tal and dragged him from the room. One of the drows kicked open a wooden door and dragged him outside. Tal took in his surroundings; the village was made up of stone buildings, all with thatched roofs. Here and there, the dark-haired elves walked around, but stopped to look at the youth as he was dragged through the village.

Tal noticed that there were no children and only a few women. The women were dressed the same as the men, they all wore the same dark green leggings and jerkins. Most of the buildings seemed abandoned and there were far too many buildings for the few elves Tal could see in the small village.

"Where all the people?" asked Tal.

One of the drows leading him struck him round the back of his head, but didn't say anything. They continued to walk in silence past row upon row of deserted buildings. Finally, they passed between two large buildings. They came to the tree-line where Tal could hear the sounds of metal striking stone. It grew louder as they entered the trees. After around a hundred paces, the trees started to thin out. The sound of striking rocks had been growing the further they walked, then Tal heard the sound of muffled voices. Nothing could have prepared the youth for what he saw next.

Tal had been led into a clearing where dwarves in chains were carrying baskets of rock from the entrance of a cave. Six of the large-horned creatures stood guard with huge wooden clubs studded with silver nails. The dwarves were emptying the baskets of rocks and retuning to the cave. One of the drows pushed Tal forward.

"You will work," it snarled at the youth. The drow then talked in a guttural language. One of the large creatures ambled over, carrying a thick golden chain which it fastened to Tal's legs. It then placed its huge hand on the youth's back and pushed him towards the cave. Tal heard the two elves laughing, again.

Tal felt the hand of the creature on his back, pushing him forward. "Pick up a basket, boy," said an elderly dwarf. His silver hair and beard were streaked with dirt and he wore a filthy lion cloth. Tal looked at the old dwarf. "Pick up a basket or the ogres will kill you." The youth quickly grabbed a basket and followed the old dwarf towards the cave.

When they were out of earshot, Tal spoke. "Who are you?" he asked the old dwarf.

"My name is Tharras," he replied.

"What are you doing here?" asked Tal.

"Doing, lad," said Tharras. "We're mining steel for the drows."

"What's a drow?"

Therras stopped walking and looked at Tal. "Where are you from?" he asked.

"I'm from across the sea," replied Tal. "From a place called Sharr."

"Well, Tal from Sharr," said Therras, "you are now a prisoner of the dark elves, or drows as my people call them. Those are the fellows with the long dark hair. The big ugly ones are called ogres and they're awful mean, so keep working." Tharras started to walk into the cave mouth. Torches had been lit and were hung from the walls in golden brackets. A steady line of dwarves had been filing in and out of the cave.

"How many of you are here?" Tal asked Therras.

"There are thirty of us here, lad," he replied.

"Has anyone ever escaped?" asked Tal, dreading the answer.

"Nope," said Therras. "Never. The ogres will hunt you down and kill you if you try and run."

"What about the other dwarves?" asked Tal.

"What about them?" asked Therras.

"Have they tried to rescue you?"

"They would if they knew we were here."

"What do you mean?" asked Tal.

"The drows move us around; we never stay in one place for too long. Our people most likely think we're dead."

"What if I could get away from here; which way do I go?"

"Look, lad," said Therras. "There's no escape form the drows. If you did manage to slip away, then you have the jungle to deal with."

"Jungle?" interrupted Tal.

"The trees, boy, the trees; that's the jungle."

"I can handle that," said Tal.

"No," said Therras, shaking his head. "With no weapons, you wouldn't last half a day; there are creatures in there that will kill you. Wolves and bears don't scare me," said Tal.

"I don't know what a wolf is," said Therras, "but the great stripped cat of the jungle can kill a man in less than a minute. Now let's keep working; otherwise, we'll be fed to the ogres."

Tal lost count of the number of times he walked in and out of the cave, his arm and legs ached and he stank of sweat. He was just about to head back inside when a horn blew. All the dwarf prisoners dropped their baskets and sat down on the floor.

"What's happening?" asked Tal.

"We're done for the day," said Therras. "They will bring us food then take us back to the holding cell until morning."

"How long have you been a prisoner?" asked Tal.

"I don't know how long I've been here, I lost count after five years," said Therras. "But I've been here longer than most, so long as you work, you will be fed and kept alive. Sit down, lad, and rest. The food will be here soon."

Derrel had dressed swiftly, donning the kilt and vest, but he still wore his own boots. He ran after Darumi. Fifty warriors sat on war birds as Derrel ran into the grounds of the chief's lodge. Two war birds stood unmounted. As he and Darumi approached, the birds squatted to the floor, allowing the two men to step into the saddle.

"Grip the bird with your thighs," said Darumi, "and do not drag on the reins, they don't like it. Use your legs to guide him in the direction you want to go."

Derrel nodded his understanding then Darumi let out a war cry and the birds started to run. Derrel was an experienced horse man and had fought many a mounted battle, but he wasn't ready for the power and the speed of the bird. Twice, he nearly fell from the bird's back as it changed direction. It took Derrel around thirty minutes to get the hang of riding, then it started to feel natural to him. Trees whizzed past the riders as they charged through the jungle. Darumi had set a fast pace but the birds seemed tireless, their long legs taking great strides soon covered the distance to the docks. The riders reined in their mounts, and Derrel was the first to dismount. The scene that greeted him was total devastation of the ships and the dock.

Derrel ran across the soft sand towards the blackened timbers, calling out his brother's name. "Tal, are you here? Tal, where are you, please?" Derrel scanned the black and burnt bodies. Was one of these his brother? It was impossible to tell; they were all burnt beyond recognition.

"Over here," yelled one of the dwarves. Derrel looked up the beach; some twenty paces away lay another body. Derrel sprinted to where the dwarves were inspecting the body. Dropping to his knees, he watched as one of them was just removing the remains of an arrow from the dead man's chest. The dwarf removed the jerking from the body, Derrel recognised the body of Captain Renshaw. His heart sank, as he recognised Tal's jerking

"Drows," said one of the dwarfs.

"Drows?" asked Derrel.

"And ogres," said the dwarf, pointing at some huge footprints in the sand.

Derrel stood and followed the tracks to the start of the jungle. "They went this way," he yelled, running back for his mount.

"Wait," called Darumi, grabbing a hold of the reins. "It will do no good; the drows are impossible to find."

"I have to try," said Derrel. "Tal could still be alive."

"No, my friend," said Darumi. "The drows do not let anyone live."

Derrel stepped down from the bird and drew his arming sword from his back. "Get out of my way, someone left that jerkin on the captain's body. It must be Tal," he said in an ice-cold voice.

Darumi took a step back. "I feel your pain," he said, "but you could ride around for days without seeing any sign of a drow; you don't even know which way they've gone. We should head back and talk with my father, he will decide what we should do."

Derrel lifted his sword, pointing it at Darumi. "I'm going to find my brother or at least avenge his death, and I swear to Ristus that I will kill every drow in this accursed land."

"Then I'm truly sorry," said Darumi, nodding his head.

"For what?" asked Derrel. The world went black as Derrel fell face-first to the sand. Behind him, one of the dwarves lowered his sickle axe. He had struck the sergeant on the back of the head with the axe shaft.

Chapter Eighteen

The winter had been harsh and bleak in Carthage, reports of food shortages had been brought to Tyrin's attention by his council. The king had ordered food to be sent out from the royal warehouses to keep the populace fed, ravens had been arriving from duchies informing the king that this winter had been a particular bad one and that shipments of food and supplies were struggling to make it through.

The days and weeks had rolled on by, the whole of Carthage had been waiting for news on their new expectant queen and the birth of her baby. That day had come towards winter's end; the sun had been shining, lifting the freezing temperature slightly. The sky had been blue and cloudless when the royal herald had announced to the whole city that Prince Obrien had been born and that the queen and her son were both in great health.

The king had ordered three days of celebrations to mark the birth of his son. Ravens were sent out to all dukes and barons; they were ordered to attend the palace in Carthage in the spring to acknowledge the birth of the young prince and swear elegance to him as the rightful heir to the throne. Finally, the raven had been sent to High Castle requesting that one of the master mages come and bestow a blessing on the young prince as was customary.

It had been Lady Davira that had attended. Tyrin and his wife had made her welcome.

"I would have thought that Elazar would have been the one

to attend," said Tyrin.

Davira bowed. "The Master Elazar sends his apologies, he has matters at High Castle that he needs to see to personally. We are focusing most of our resources on finding a way to stop the curse of Sagoth coming true."

Tyrin nodded his understanding and turned to his wife. "My dear, would you please get our son so that the good Lady Davira can bestow her blessing upon him."

Emelia walked over to a beautifully crafted bassinet that had been crafted from a white wood. White silk and lace adorned the bassinet of the prince. Emelia's long honey-blonde hair fell forward as she leaned over where the new-born baby lay, happily cooing away to himself. Emelia lifted the prince from the bassinet, he had been wrapped in soft white woollen blankets.

"May I present to you my son, Prince Obrien," said Emelia.

Davira smiled. "May I?" she asked, reaching out her arms.

"But of course," replied Emelia, handing over her son and smoothing down her blue silk dress.

Davira looked into the blue eyes of the young prince and smiled at the queen. "He looks like you," said Davira. "He even has your eyes. He will grow up to be handsome, tall and strong."

Emelia smiled. "Thank you."

"With your permission," said Davira, looking at Tyrin. The king nodded his head. Davira laid the infant back in the bassinet and unwrapped the blanket, the baby started cooing louder as the mage ran her hands over his small body while whispering an incantation. Davira released the spell which contained the blessing.

"It is done, Your Majesties," she said. "And I'm happy to say that the child is fit and well."

Emelia breathed a sigh of relief as did Tyrin. A light tapping came at the door of the king and queen's apartments.

"Enter," said Tyrin in a stern voice. The large oak door opened and General Kaylin stepped into the room and bowed to the king and queen and then to Lady Davira. Tyrin knew why his friend had interrupted them.

"My love," he said to Emelia, "would you please excuse us?"

"Of course, my love," she replied. Emelia took up the young prince and excused herself from the room. As Emelia left, Tyrin looked at Davira. "My lady, the general and I would like it if you could contact Lady Shamari on Rainoa. We are most keen to know if our men and cargo arrived safely."

Davira bowed her head. "I will try, Your Majesty," she replied. "First, I will need a bowl and some water."

Tyrin went to the door and called for a servant to bring what the mage had asked for. Within a few moments, a large bowl and a jug of water had been placed on the table in the king's apartments. Closing her eyes, Davira started to once more whisper words that the two men in the room could not understand. She started to make small gestures with her fingers, the water in the bowl seemed to shimmer and the image of a woman with dark hair appeared.

"Greetings, my sister," said Davira.

The image of Shamari smiled. "It is good to see you. How goes it at High Castle?"

"All is well," replied Davira.

"And what of the gateway in Carthage, is that ready?"

"It is," replied Davira. "How goes the gate in Rainoa?"

"I am still working tirelessly," replied Shamari. "It is taking all my power to ready things at this end. Being the only user of magic is taking its toll on my powers, I should be ready in a few more months."

Tyrin coughed. "My lady, if you could enquire as to our ships?"

"Yes, Your Majesty," said Davira. "I am with His Majesty King Tyrin," said Davira. "Might I enquire as to the ships the king sent? Did they arrive safely with the cargo?"

"Yes, they arrived safely and the cargo was delivered. Chief Detas is most pleased with the steel the king sent."

Tyrin stepped forward and looked at the image of the mage in the water.

"Have the ships started their return journey?" he asked.

"No, Your Highness, they have not," she replied.

"Why not?" Tyrin asked. "Is there a problem?"

"I'm afraid that I'm the bearer of bad news, Your Majesty," said Shamari. "The cargo was delivered but as the gold was being loaded, the ships came under attack from the drows."

"Drows?" asked Kaylin, stepping forward.

"They are a race of elves," said Shamari, "not at all like the elves of the Great Forest. The dwarves here call them drows; it means Dark Elf."

"My sons?" asked Kaylin, a touch of fear sounding in his voice.

"Derrel had accompanied me to deliver the cargo to the dwarves," she said. "Tal had stayed behind with the other soldiers."

"What aren't you telling me?" snapped Kaylin, anger replacing the fear in his voice.

Shamari lowered her gaze. "I'm afraid that all at the ships were killed; no one survived."

"No!" cried Kaylin. "This cannot be, not my son." Pain ran through his chest which caused him to stagger.

Tyrin grabbed the general and eased him to one of the couches in the room. "Kaylin, what's wrong?"

"I'm fine," said Kaylin, waving the king away.

Tyrin returned to the image of Shamari. "Did Chief Detas receive my gift?" he asked.

"Yes, Your Majesty, as I said the steel was delivered safely."

"No!" stormed Tyrin. "I sent a separate gift for the chief, I had a golden war hammer crafted for him as a special gift."

"I'm sorry to inform you, Your Majesty, that Detas did not receive such a gift."

Tyrin slammed his hand down on the table; the image in the bowl shifted.

"Please, Your Majesty," said Davira, "it is quite difficult to sustain this spell."

"My apologies," said Tyrin. "How long until the gateway is ready?" Tyrin asked.

"As I said, Your Majesty, it will be a few more months. It is taking all my power to construct the necessary spells for the gateways to align."

"I would consider this a personal favour if you could complete the gateway sooner."

"I will try, Your Majesty," replied Shamari.

"How is Derrel?" asked Kaylin from where he was sitting.

"He is well, General. Considering what has happened, he has sworn to kill every drow here in Rainoa to avenge his brother."

It was Tyrin who spoke next. "I would like you to tell Sergeant Mendez that he will wait until he hears from me, he is to aid you in any way possible in the completion of the gateway."

"Your Majesty," said Kaylin.

"Once the gateway is complete, I will send a full detachment through to aid him."

"It will be as you command, Your Majesty," said Shamari. The image faded as Davira released the spell.

Tyrin went back to Kaylin's side. "I will send for the medic, my friend, just sit still."

Chapter Nineteen

Urag had been outraged at being summoned by this human in black; he had vowed to skin the black-garbed man alive and that his screams would echo through the mountains for a thousand years. Everyone would remember his cries, and no one would ever think to summon the orc ruler again.

Urag had marched every orc through the mountains to witness what would happen to any that tried to stand in his way; thousands of orcs had arrived at the Dark Fortress, their screams echoing throughout the ruins. A lone figure sat crossed-legged in the centre of what was once the keep.

A dark hood obscured his face, the powerful figure of Urag pushed his way through the amassing orcs to stand before the lone figure.

"Who are you to summon me?" snarled Urag. The man did not move, nor did he respond. Urag's irritation exploded into anger. "Kill him," roared the orc leader.

Orcs ran forward to hack and slash at the seated man; he did not move or flinch as sword axe and spear were thrust towards his body. He merely sat there as the blades met with an unseen barrier. After a short time, Urag called a stop to the attack. The orc warriors backed away from the seated man. Urag took a tentative step forward, the seated man reached an arm up and pulled back his hood, fixing his dark eyes on Urag. The orc leader shuddered as he felt the power emanating from this mysterious man.

"Now that you have seen my power," said a deep resonating voice, "it is time to get to work."

"Who are you?" demanded Urag.

"I am Kadius of High Castle, servant to Sagoth."

At the mention of the dark god's name, some of the orcs screeched and looked around nervously.

"Sagoth fell," said Urag. "The humans and their allies defeated him."

"The Lord Sagoth will rise again," said Kadius. "We must ready everything for his return. You have started to gather his armies, now we must ensure that the armies know victory. We will start by rebuilding the fortress and then we will train your army."

"How will we keep this from the humans and from the other mages of this land? They will see the fortress," snarled Urag.

"No, my new friend," said Kadius. "They will not, for the spell that protects me will hide what we are doing here. Should anyone pass this way, they will still see a ruin. Once I cast the spell, no one see what we are building. The fortress shall be more glorious than before. I will speed up time within the range of the spell, you will select the strongest warriors to breed with the females to ensure that the next generation of orcs is stronger than the one before. Now, let us prepare for our master's return."

The snows had begun to thaw, and the promise of spring hung in the air. General Kaylin had been growing more and more inpatient for the magical gateway to be built. He had vowed to join his son on Rainoa to avenge Tal's death.

Tyrin had gone to Kaylin in his private rooms one evening where he found his friend more than a little drunk.

"I am truly sorry for your loss, my friend," said Tyrin. "I

cannot imagine the loss you feel for your son nor would I want to."

Kaylin sat slumped in a chair, nursing a goblet of red wine. "Tal was a good lad," he said, his words slurring. "I know he had a mischievous nature, but he was a good-hearted boy."

"Your sons have done you proud," said Tyrin. "Derrel is one of the finest men I have ever known."

Kaylin drained the goblet. "You have always been like a son to me," he said, refilling his goblet. "I'm proud of you, boy. Ever since the loss of your father fifteen years ago, you have had to be strong."

Tyrin smiled at his friend. "I had you to help me," he said. "I would not be the king I am today without your aid, my friend."

Kaylin smiled warmly. "What is it you want, Tyrin?" he asked.

"I want to ride to the Great Forest and speak with Alinar to ask him about the drows. Maybe he can help us understand them."

Kaylin drained the goblet once more. "What is there to understand; they killed my boy, and our men. They have taken that which you swore to guard with your very life, we need to go to Rainoa, avenge my son and retrieve that dam gem."

Kaylin tried to stand, but his legs wouldn't obey him; he slumped back into the chair, the goblet falling from his hand and clanking on the floor. The old general was asleep, he had taken to drinking upon hearing of his youngest son's death.

Tyrin walked to the bed and took one of the woollen blankets and covered his friend.

"We will avenge your son," he said to the sleeping man.

Derrel awoke; his head was pounding. The room was lit by a

single candle, and the bed he lay on was soft and his body was covered by a thin cotton blanket. He groaned as he tried to sit up.

"Lay still," said a soft voice. "You've been unconscious for a few hours now." Shamari came into view. She was once again dressed in the blue robes of the mages.

"Where am I?" he asked her.

"You are in my quarters," she told him. "Darumi and his men brought you back here from the beach."

"Who hit me?" he asked.

"Does it matter?" she replied, mopping his brow with a cool damp cloth.

"It matters to me," he said coldly.

Shamari's face hardened. "Whoever hit you did you a favour," she told him. "If you would have run off into that jungle, you would probably be dead now."

"You underestimate me," he said more harshly than he had intended. "I have told you there is nothing that bleeds that I cannot kill."

Shamari sat on the bed beside him. "I know you must be feeling angry," she said, "but what would it accomplish if you ran off into the jungle and by some chance found the drows? What would you do, take them all on?"

Derrel gritted his teeth.

"I know you are a great swordsman," said Shamari, "but I doubt even you could take on all the drows and their ogres."

Derrel seemed to relax a little. "He is..." Derrel faltered, "he was my brother and I failed to protect him." tears came to Derrel's eyes.

"No," said Shamari. "There was no way you could have known." She lent down and kissed him. Derrel's arm encircled her waist and gently he pulled her towards him.

Once more, Derrel found himself alone. Shamari was nowhere to be seen. He sat up on the bed, the room was rather resplendent in the daylight. The bed frame was made of gold, and thick rugs had been strewn across the polished stone floor. At one end of the room stood a table with what looked like a bronze mirror on it. Derrel threw back his blankets and walked across to the mirror; it was not bronze, it was made from gold that had been polished to a mirror finish. Everywhere he looked in the room, he could see gold, from the hinges on the door to the window frames. The gold in this room alone would allow him to live in luxury for the rest of his life.

"And I would trade it all for you, Tal," he said aloud. The pain of losing his brother hit him harder than the blow to his head. Anger threatened to overwhelm him, but he quelled it. A light knock came at the door and Derrel suddenly realised he was naked.

"Just a moment," he called, returning to the bed and covering his body with the blanket.

The door opened slowly and a young dwarf woman entered. She had short dark hair that was cut just above the shoulder, and she wore a simple yellow cotton dress, in the style that Derrel had seen all the women wear.

"Would you like breakfast?" she asked, averting her eyes from him and blushing.

"That would be nice," answered Derrel. The young girl bowed and quickly left the room. Derrel turned his attention back to the table with the golden mirror, fresh clothes had been left for him along with a pair of the ankle-high boots that the dwarves wore. Quickly, he donned the black kilt and black vest and slipped on the black leather boots, then he made his way to the kitchen for breakfast.

After a substantial meal of eggs, bacon and fresh bread, the young sergeant made his way through the house that Shamari was using. The young servant women giggled as he walked past them, Finally, he came to what looked like a study room that had been furnished with thick padded couches and an ornate table and chairs. Derrel noted he had not seen a fireplace in any of the rooms, yet the house was still warm. Shamari came walking into the study, carrying a large leather-bound book.

"You're awake," she said, smiling, her blue mages' robe flowing as she walked to the table and placed the book down. "How do you feel?" she asked.

"My head is still a little sore, but I feel fine," he replied.

"I have some news," she said, gesturing to one of the chairs near the table. Derrel took a seat. "I communed with my sister mage Davira this morning. The gateway in Sharr is ready."

"That is good news," answered Derrel.

"I also informed King Tyrin and your father of what has transpired here," she said, her voice softening. She noticed the look of pain on the young man's face. "The king has ordered you not to pursue the drows; he has said he will send through soldiers to help you track them down when the gate here is complete."

Derrel gritted his teeth, his breathing deepening. "If that is what my king has ordered, then so be it," he said. "Please excuse me, my lady," he said, standing. "I wish to be alone." Derrel turned to leave.

"Sergeant," called Shamari. Derrel paused in the doorway, but did not look back at her. "I am truly sorry for the loss of your brother," she said. "I will do my best to get the gateway open and working."

Derrel merely nodded and left the room.

Chapter Twenty

Spring had arrived in Sharr with the promise of a good summer to come. The dukes and barons had arrived, and a great celebration had been held in the young prince's honour. Each duke and baron had knelt before the queen who held her babe in her arms; they had all sworn to serve the young prince and acknowledged him as heir to the kingdom. But still rumours circulated that some of the nobles were still unhappy of the king's marriage to a market traders' daughter.

Again, the Duke of Movale seemed to be the most vocal on the point. He had attended the celebration with his wife and his two oversized daughters. General Kaylin also noticed the two young dark-haired men dressed in black leather that had accompanied the duke; both were in their mid-twenties and had beady eyes and hooked noses. Kaylin remembered the duke's cousin Kainos, the former captain of the watch; the two young men were undoubtedly his sons.

As Kaylin walked past the fat duke, he had called out to the general, "My dear fellow, how are you?"

Kaylin had bowed in greeting. "I am very well, my Lord Duke, and it is good of you to attend the crowned prince's celebration." Kaylin noticed the look of annoyance that set on the duke's face at the mention of the prince.

"May I introduce you to my two nephews," said Cedric. The two young men nodded their heads to the general. "The young man on your right is Deacon Tybost and the young man on your left is Marcelo Tybost."

"It is a pleasure to meet you," said Marcelo. "My brother and I have heard so much about you and your son. Is he in attendance?" Marcelo looked around the hall of the palace. "It is said that his skills with a blade are legendary." The young man continued to look around, not meeting the old general's gaze.

Kaylin's eyes narrowed, and his jaw clenched. "My son is away on the king's business. He has been gone now for almost a year, but please be assured that I will inform him that you were asking after him." General Kaylin inclined his head once more and then left. He glanced back once to see Cedric and his two nephews having a heated exchange.

The old general had known that the former captain's sons would seek revenge for the death of their father at some point, even though the king had forbidden it. The rest of the night's festivities went without incident.

The snows had melted, giving way to spring and a sign that warmer weather was on its way. Tyrin and Kaylin readied themselves for the journey south to the Great Forest of the elves.

General Kaylin had been withdrawn after learning of the death of his youngest son, Tal. Tyrin suspected that the only thing keeping his friend going now was the prospect of the gateway being opened and avenging his son's death. Tyrin had gathered the king's guard to accompany him south. Five hundred of the king's finest soldiers all dressed in their silver armour with black leather leggings their black cloaks fluttering in the breeze, the sunlight glinted from the silver helms of the soldiers as General Kaylin rode his chestnut mare, inspecting the troops.

Tyrin's steel grey stallion started to prance as he rode towards the waiting soldiers, the stallion was snorting and swooshing his tail and his steps were exaggerated to the point of being comical.

"The men are ready, Your Majesty," said Kaylin as the king approached. "Is there something wrong with your mount, my king?" asked Kaylin.

"No," answered Tyrin. "He's just showing off, he does this whenever I wear full armour. I think that he thinks it impresses me." Tyrin lent forward in the saddle. "Shadow, behave, you're making a show of yourself. You look ridiculous."

The horse took no notice of its rider and continued to prance around as the king made his speech. "Today, men, we make history. We will be the first humans to walk in the Great Forest of the elves. King Alinar has invited us personally. We are to establish a trade between our two nations."

The men started to tap their sabres on their shields, which made Shadow's prancing grow even more ridiculous.

"The ride will be long and it will take you from your loved ones," said Tyrin, "as it will take me from mine, but this will secure a greater future for our kingdom."

The five hundred soldiers all pointed their sabres to the sky, the cry of long live the king came in unison. Shadow reared up on to his hind legs, his front legs thrashing at the air.

"Move out," bellowed Kaylin.

The column of soldiers moved out, heading towards the planes of Varith. Tyrin brought his wayward mount under control. "Do behave yourself, Shadow," he said in a pained voice. "It's a long ride and all your fancy prancing will see you left at the first farm we come across. I'll tell the farmer to hitch you to a plough and you can work the fields until I come back from this trip."

The horse stopped immediately, his ears going flat to his head. "Good," said Tyrin. "Now we understand each other." He touched his heels to the horse but Shadow refused to move.

"All right," said Tyrin, leaning forward in his saddle. "You can show off to the elves when we get to the Great Forest."

Shadow's ears flicked forward and he set off at a slow trot, following the five hundred soldiers and the supply wagons as they started towards the Great Forest.

Derrel had been in the dwarf city of Udila now for four months and he had grown accustomed to the leather kilt and vest. He had even adopted the short cropped hair of the dwarves; this had helped with the flies. He now understood the reason the dwarves wore their hair short. Derrel had spent every moment he could with Shamari, he had even moved from the accommodation that had been given to him, and now shared living quarters with her. Each night he would share her bed and every morning he would wake alone.

He knew Shamari would be working on the gateway. Derrel noticed that Shamari looked more tired each evening when she returned and that she now always wore her mages robes.

"I am worried that you are pushing yourself too hard, my lady," he had said one night.

Shamari smiled at him. "I am trying to complete the gate, my love. You have been away from your home for too long."

Derrel had taken her in his arms. "You are my home now, my lady, I will stay where you stay."

She had kissed him deeply. "There is something I must tell you." Derrel looked at the woman he loved with a growing concern. Shamari slowly unfastened the front of her blue robe to expose her now swelling stomach. "I am with child, you are to be a father."

Derrel stepped forward and placed his hand on Shamari's

stomach.

"How long until the baby is due?" he asked.

"Between four and five months."

"Then we must marry, I will ask Detas to perform the ceremony."

"Wait," Shamari said, "I am almost a century old. My magic will see me outlive you and the child growing inside me if he is not blessed by magic. I could not bear to watch you both grow old."

"Then it is a boy," said Derrel, smiling.

Shamari met his gaze and nodded her head. "Yes, your son is strong and growing fast."

"No matter how much time we have together, I will love and cherish every day with you." Derrel took Shamari in his arms and kissed her longingly.

The journey south to the Great Forest had been a pleasant one. General Kaylin had been more like his old self; the discipline of the men was the finest in all the king's army, the men obeying and carrying out Kaylin's orders with precise efficiency.

Tyrin had taken his army through each village and town where he had been warmly greeted by barons and dukes alike, but he chose each night to sleep with his army, turning down invitations to stop in great houses and manors, all to the disappointment of the nobles. After weeks of travel, their destination was in sight. The vastness of the forest was hard to believe for anyone that had never seen it. The forest stretched as far as the eye could see; a blanket of green that stretched to the horizon.

"How long do you think it will take us to reach the borders of the forest?" Tyrin asked Kaylin.

"We should reach their borders tomorrow, Your Majesty," the general replied.

"Then I think we should make camp here," said Tyrin, looking up at the sun. "I judge it to be around midday. If we rest the men and the mounts, we should arrive fresh tomorrow to meet our hosts."

General Kaylin bowed in the saddle. "It will be as you say, Your Majesty." Kaylin turned the chestnut gelding and rode back to the advancing soldiers. He started to bark out orders to make camp. Within two hours, the camp had been set, the cooking fires lit and the king's tent had been pitched.

Tyrin sat in one of the chairs in his tent. He had removed his silver armour and was now dressed in a simple grey leggings and jerkin. Kaylin came into the tent carrying a plate of bread and cheese with a slab of beef for the king.

"It was good of the farmer at the last settlement to provide the beef for the men," said Kaylin, handing the plate to Tyrin.

"Yes, I agree, fresh meet is always a welcome after eating trail rations." Tyrin noticed the bags under his friend's eyes. "How are you?" he asked the general.

"I would like to say all is well, Your Majesty, but I have lost my son and nothing can bring him back. My eldest is half a world away and my heart aches to see his return."

"I wish I could unburden your pain, my friend. I have only been away from my son and his mother for a couple of weeks and my heart yearns for them."

Kaylin sat in one of the chairs, letting out a deep breath and fixed his gaze to the king. "I will retire after this mission," he said to Tyrin. "I will go to my estates and grow old and fat, I think." There was a smile upon his face, but Tyrin saw no happiness within the smile. "Derrel will take my place as your champion, I doubt that any would wish to challenge for the position."

Tyrin lent forward, placing a hand on his friend's knee. "If that is your wish, my friend, then so be it, but what will you do to occupy your time?"

Kaylin smiled again, this time there seemed to be some happiness in it. "With His Majesty's permission, I would request the loan of that stallion of yours. I have never known a horse like him, I would like to put him to stud and see if I can breed a more intelligent war mount for your armies."

Tyrin let out a soft chuckle. "Now that would be a sight to see, an army prancing into battle on the backs of horses like Shadow." Both men started to laugh at the thought of the sight.

The next morning, the soldiers broke camp. The supply wagons and horses set off on the final part of the journey to the Great Forest of the elves. The sun was steadily rising in the east, bringing with it the promise of a warm day. The trip south had gone by without incident, there had been no attempt by bandits to attack the supply wagons, but then again who would be stupid enough to attack a supply train with five hundred of the king's finest soldiers following it?

In the distance, the Great Forest loomed. the seemingly endless ocean of trees growing larger and larger as they rode towards it. By midday, they had reached the borders of the elves. General Kaylin called a halt to the soldiers and supply wagons and ordered the camp to be made. Soldiers hurried to carry out his orders as the wagons were drawn up into a semi-circle, tents were pitched and cooking fires were lit. Kaylin sat atop his mount, watching with pride as the men prepared the camp.

A horn blew from the trees. All activity ceased as the soldiers looked to where the horn blast had come from. Twenty tall figures dressed in burnished golden armour stepped forth from the trees, their white cloaks billowed out behind them in the soft breeze. Each elven soldier had a quiver of arrows and carried an ornate long bow. Belted at their side, the soldiers carried a slim-blade sword sharpened down one edge like a sabre, but these blades were straight with a slight belly to the blade near the bottom.

Tyrin nudged Shadow forward; the large grey stallion took full advantage of the attention. With all eyes on him and his rider, the horse's prancing was even more ridiculous than normal.

"Really, Shadow," said Tyrin, trying to stifle a laugh. Shadow whooshed his tail and nodded his head all while snorting. Tyrin gently pulled on the reins some ten paces from the elves, all of whom had a bemused look on their faces.

"Greetings, King Tyrin," said the lead elf. "My name is Elmon. My lord and king offers you his warmest welcome. He has permitted you safe entry into our lands, and King Alinar has given permission for ten of your company to accompany you."

Tyrin nodded. "I thank you, Elmon. You will have to excuse my horse, Shadow has a flavour for the theatricals." The stallion's ears went flat to his head at the mention of his name. Elmon nodded as if he understood.

"When you are ready, Your Majesty, you and your men can follow us back where His Highness is waiting for you."

Chapter Twenty-One

Elmon led his company of elves and Tyrin into the forest. A sense of calm fell over the riders as they followed the escorts, even Shadow walked at a calmer pace.

"This is a truly beautiful place," Tyrin said to Elmon.

The elf inclined his head slightly and smiled.

"It has been our home ever since I can remember," said the blond elf. "The magic of the land is strong here and feeds us, and the trees."

"Why have you never sought to trade with other nations?" asked Tyrin.

"The forest has always provided everything we need."

"Then why has your king asked for this meeting between our two nations?"

"That is something you must discuss with my king, but you should know that the elven council has discussed this at great length, and that not all agreed to this meeting. Some feel that we should depend on the magic of the forest to sustain our people, but others have agreed that a change is needed to help with the continued survival of our race."

The demeanour of Elmon seemed to change, his face betraying his emotions. "I am saying too much, this is for you and King Alinar to discuss."

Tyrin was about to ask another question but noticed a change in the trees; gone was the normal size of the trees, the trees around them seemed to have tripled in size, stretching towards the heavens.

"By Ristus," said Tyrin, "those are the biggest trees I have ever seen."

Elmon smiled. "This is the start of the heart of the forest. Some of these trees are thousands of years old, their roots run deep and draw the magic from the land that feeds the forest."

If Tyrin had been impressed by the size of the trees at the edge of the elven city, nothing could have prepared him for what he saw next. Elmon led the party of elves and men into the elven city hidden within the Great Forest. The trees here were enormous and the very trees themselves seemed to have been made into the buildings for the elves. Tyrin sat atop Shadow, his mouth hung open as he drank in the beauty of his surroundings.

Tyrin knew that the elves used magic that was derived from the land, and now he could see that magic put to use. Some of the trees had leaves of silver and gold shining like lanterns that cast a warm and peaceful glow to the forest. Tyrin turned to Kaylin, he too was sat with the same expression on his face; a look of wonderment and bewilderment.

"This is truly breath-taking," said Tyrin. "I can see why you would want to hide this from the rest of the world."

"His Majesty is too gracious," said Elmon, bringing the party to a halt. "Please dismount, my king approaches," he said, gesturing to his right.

Tyrin looked to where Elmon had gestured and saw the tall blond figure of Alinar walking towards him. The elf king wore simple white leggings and jerkin that hung past his waist, a small golden circlet adorned his head and a broad smile showed on his face as he walked towards them.

"Greetings, my friend," said Alinar, taking hold of Tyrin's hand in a warrior's grip. "It is good to see you again."

"And you," replied Tyrin.

"We have heard of your marriage and of the birth of your son." Tyrin looked shocked which amused the elf king. "We may live within the forest, my friend, but we have ways and means of finding out what goes on in the world."

Kaylin let out a chuckle. "You will have to forgive His Majesty," said the old general. "He has been caught up looking after his new son and wife that he has forgotten that the world lives on without his say so."

Tyrin gave his old friend a pained look, much to the amusement of the elf king.

"Come along, my friend," said Alinar. "You must be tired and hungry after your journey. Let us eat and drink and we can talk of family life and the future of our two nations."

Tyrin and his men had been led to a huge tree that was hundreds feet in diameter. A doorway had been made in the base of the trunk which led into a room that had been carved inside the tree. To one side of the room stood a spiral staircase. Alinar led Tyrin and his men up the stairs, showing each one of them a room where they were told they could rest. The rooms were simple, all the furniture inside had been made from the wood of the tree. Fresh clothing in the style of the elves' white leggings and a white jerkin had been laid out for them.

"Please," said Alinar, gesturing with a sweep of his hand, "our home is yours while you stay. Rest a while and one of my people will come and collect you for the banquet to be thrown in your honour."

It had been around two hours when Tyrin heard a light knocking on the door. "Enter," said Tyrin and the door opened.

A young child-like elf girl stood in the doorway; her voice

was soft and melodious.

"His Highness King Alinar askes that you accompany me, I am to take you to the banquet." Tyrin inclined his head and followed after the young girl.

Tables had been set out in the forest in a half circle. Upon them lay all manner of food from wild pheasant to venison. At the centre of the table sat King Alinar, beside him stood an empty chair. The young girl led Tyrin to the empty seat. Alinar stood as Tyrin approached and extended his hand.

"Welcome, my friend, please be seated and we will dine as friends tonight and discuss the future of our two kingdoms."

The young girl lent forward and embraced the king. "May I present to you my daughter, Princess Almera. It is to her you owe the thanks for this meeting; she has been most persuasive in allowing you to come here."

Tyrin bowed deeply to the young girl. "Then you have my profound thanks, Princess," said Tyrin, smiling warmly at the girl.

"Tell me of your son," said Almera. "I am curious to know about him."

Tyrin smiled at the mention of his son. "He is a fine boy," said Tyrin. "He is now four months old and growing strong."

"I would like to meet him," said Almera. She turned to her father. "Could we journey to Carthage so I can see the baby, Father?"

Alinar smiled. "One day, perhaps, but you now need to excuse yourself while I discuss terms with His Majesty.",

Almera bowed to the two kings and excused herself.

"Your daughter is lovely," said Tyrin. "How old is she?" he asked.

"Almera has just entered her one hundredth year."

Tyrin almost choked on the mouthful of wine he had just drunk. "One hundred!" he exclaimed. "She doesn't look a day over sixteen."

Alinar chuckled at Tyrin's reaction. "You have to understand," said Alinar, "that elves age differently to humans. Almera is still a child to us; she may be a hundred in your years but to an elf a hundred years is but a blink of an eye."

"Why is your daughter so interested in my son?" asked Tyrin.

Alinar gave an uneasy smile. "One of the reasons I asked you here has to do with our children. Take a look around." He gestured his hand in a sweeping motion. "Tell me how many children you see."

Tyrin looked around as the elves and humans ate. He counted around twenty-five young-looking elves that looked the same age as the king's daughter. "You see," said Alinar, "we have not had a new birth here for half a century. Although we are long-lived, my people are a dying race. We number around ten thousand and with fewer births, I fear we will not be here much longer. That is why we came to your call to arms. The wars of men do not interest us, but when the orcs awoke Sagoth, that put all our lives in peril. Our fates are now entwined for should Sagoth indeed be reborn once more, he will send out his legions to destroy you and your kind, then he will turn his attention on the rest of the world. I fear that we would be the next to be attacked. Sagoth was once a god, but he was cast from the heavens to dwell with the races of this world. Your god Ristus defeated him in battle so for Sagoth to be able to challenge Ristus once more, he must destroy the source of his power which comes from the worship of men."

"And what of your god?" asked Tyrin.

Alinar crossed his arms over his chest and lowered his head.

"Dianus our goddess and god of the land was slain by Sagoth. He tricked the other gods into an alliance to defeat Ristus, but Sagoth failed. As Dianus passed, she released her essence into this forest and the land, giving us protection and great longevity, but the cost of a long life is countered by the loss of not bearing many offspring."

"What is it that you are proposing?" asked Tyrin.

"I have held council with the elders since my return from the Black Mountains on how we can overcome this problem."

"And what is the conclusion you have come to?" Tyrin asked.

"A union between our people."

"A union?" asked Tyrin. "What exactly are you proposing?"

"I am proposing that my daughter marry your son when he comes of age, uniting our two people. This has been discussed at length and Almera has agreed to the marriage."

"But my son is still feeding from his mother's breast and your daughter is a hundred years old."

Alinar let out a good-humoured laugh. "By the time your son reaches his twentieth birthday, Almera will look the same then as she looks now. She will look as if time has stood still."

"This is something I must put to my council too, Your Highness," said Tyrin. "A decision like this is not to be taken lightly, and I must talk with my wife on the matter of betrothing our son to your daughter."

"Think on this," said Alinar. "Should our children be bound together in marriage, their children will have a greater life span, ensuring that the Degarre name continues to rule the land and sits on the throne at Carthage."

This seemed to please Tyrin. "I need to ask you something about elves."

"But of course," said Alinar. "What is it that you wish to know?"

"I sent a ship to the new land across the eastern sea."

Alinar nodded his head. "I have heard that you have discovered dwarves living there."

"Yes," said Tyrin, "but we have also recently found out that elves live in this new land."

"Elves?" asked Alinar, looking concerned.

"Yes," continued Tyrin. "The dwarves call them drows."

Alinar's eyes went wide. Once again, he crossed his arms over his chest and uttered Dianus's name. "The dark ones."

"What?" asked Tyrin.

"The drows or the dark ones as we call them turned to the worship of Sagoth upon the death of Dianus. We had thought that all of the dark ones had been killed, we drove out the dark ones that converted to the worship of Sagoth and hunted them down and slayed them. Have you had contact with these dark ones?"

"In a way, yes; they attacked my men, killing all but the general's eldest son. They then fled. Elazar and the mages are constructing a magical gateway between our two lands to enable trade with the dwarves."

"Be careful, my friend, for should the dark one discover the gate, it would allow them to join with the orcs."

Tyrin lent in close to Alinar. "What of the gem?" he asked.

The elf king stiffened in his seat. "The gem has been placed deep within our borders. I chose twenty of my finest warriors to guard it day and night, the accursed thing lies within a box made from the purest gold. We used the magic of the forest to grow a tree, inside that tree trunk we placed the box to imprison it."

"A tree?" asked Tyrin. "That would take decades to grow."

"No, my friend, as I said we used the land magic to aid its

growth. The tree in human years is already a century old. The tree is tall and strong with deep roots, the gold the gem lies in combined with the magic of the land will keep it hidden."

"This is truly a magical place," said Tyrin, lifting his wine goblet. "Come, my friend, let us toast to the future and the pending joining of our two houses."

Chapter Twenty-Two

Tyrin woke to the sound of a gentle tapping on the door. Sitting up in the bed, he looked around. His room was plain and simple, the furnishings were made from wood, the table seemed to have grown from the very wall it was nestled against. Green rugs had been placed on the floor. The tapping came once more.

"Come in," called Tyrin. The door slowly opened and the Princess Almera stepped into the room and smiled.

"I trust you slept well, Your Majesty."

Tyrin smiled. "I did, thank you," he replied. "I think I may have indulged in a little too much wine last night."

"Elven wine is much stronger than what you humans are used to," she told him.

"You will get no argument from me on that, Princess," replied Tyrin, rubbing at his head. "Is General Kaylin awake yet?"

"No, he is still sleeping. I was going to wake him after I woke you."

"Please let him sleep a little longer; he hasn't been sleeping much these past few months since the loss of his son."

Almera nodded her head in understanding. "My father bids that you join him when you are ready. Food and refreshments are waiting for you." The slim blonde girl turned to leave, but Tyrin called after her.

"Princess, do you know of what your father and I discussed last night?"

The princess turned and smiled. "I do."

"And you are OK with your father's request?"

Almera's smile broadened. Tyrin was struck by how beautiful this girl was. "I am fully aware of what my father told you last night, Your Majesty, and there is something you should know."

"And that is?"

"The idea was mine," said the princess.

The look of shock was quite apparent on Tyrin's face, which made Almera chuckle.

"Now, let me ask you something; would you prefer I call you Your Majesty or Father once your son and I are married?"

Tyrin was not normally a man stuck for words, but this girl had completely shocked him. Regaining some composure, he simply said, "The choice will be yours, Princess."

Almera bowed. "Father it is, then," she said smiling, then left the room.

Tyrin had dressed in the elven clothing provided for him and had made to leave the room. He paused at the door, turned and took up his sword and belted it at his waist. King Alinar was waiting for him as he came from the tree building.

"I trust you are rested. Come, we will eat then I must talk with you on another matter."

After Tyrin and Alinar had broken their fast, the two kings wandered through the forest, home of the elves for quite some time.

"You said there was something else you wanted to discuss with me. Does something trouble you?"

"Beyond our borders to the south, there lays a desolate wasteland. Few creatures live there due to the harsh conditions, but every now and again, we get some of those creatures wandering into our forest."

"And this is a problem?" Tyrin asked.

"No," Alinar replied. "The ogres are quite docile and are only looking for food."

"I sense there is something you are not telling me."

Alinar took in a deep breath. "After we brought that accursed gem here, the ogres have become more restless, more noticeable, more aggressive. We have seen more of them pass through the forest, heading north. Normally, they would come, eat their fill and head back south, but now they do not return home."

"And you think this is something to do with the gem?" asked Tyrin.

"That I do not know," Alinar replied. Tyrin was about to ask another question when an elf came running towards the two kings. The elf stopped and bowed.

"Your Majesties, our scouts have reported ogres in the forest heading north,"

"How many?" asked the elf king.

"The scouts have reported at least twelve of them, but in their current direction they will emerge from the forest where King Tyrin's men are camped."

The four hundred and ninety men of the king's guard were waiting patiently for the king to return, the ride south had been uneventful. Talk around the campfires between the soldiers consisted of past battles and why the king had thought that he would need five hundred soldiers for a diplomatic mission. The king had even stopped in some of the towns and villages along the way to listen to some of the concerns of his people.

Groups of children had followed after the columns of soldiers, some pretending to ride imaginary horses, others having mock sword fights with sticks. All the soldiers knew that their skills as a man of war would not or should not be called upon. It was simple, escort the king to the Great Forest where he would open trade talks with the elves, then they would escort him back to Carthage. What could go wrong?

The sun had just started to set, turning the sky to a dark orange, and long shadows were being cast across the land. the attack on the camp had come without warning, a thick fog had rolled in from the south, bringing with it a sense of unease. As was normal, sentries had been placed on watch. These sentries were relieved every two hours to keep the men's senses sharp. A young soldier was the first to notice that something was wrong, the horses in the coral seemed to be skittish.

"Probably a wolf nearby," replied his comrade, throwing one of the logs at the side of the brazier into the mist and letting out a curse. "That should scare that bastard thing off."

The horses started to stamp their hooves and their snorting became louder.

"I don't think that's a wolf out there," said the first sentry, "a wolf wouldn't cause that much panic to a war mount."

The second sentry grabbed one of the burning timbers from the brazier. "By Ristus, I'll shove this up the damn thing's arse," he said, walking off to where the horses were gathered. The first sentry watched as his companion disappeared into the thickening fog. The horses continued making their panicked noises.

"Can you see anything?" shouted the first sentry. There was no answer. "Silas, come on, answer me. We only have half an hour left before our relief comes." There was still no answer.

The sentry picked up a piece of wood from the brazier. From within the fog came a dull thud, followed by a gurgling sound. "Silas, was that you?" asked the sentry. Something whizzed past the sentry's head; as it did, something warm and wet landed on his cheek. The sentry touched his finger to his cheek and looked down to see blood upon his finger.

The sentry drew his sabre with a trembling hand and turned to look at what had landed on the floor behind him. There staring back at him was the head of Silas; his face locked in an expression of fear, his mouth was open as if letting out a silent scream. Quickly, the sentry ran into the camp, shouting at the top of his voice, "We're under attack, arm yourselves."

Soldiers around the campfires quickly came to their feet, weapons in hand. Other soldiers came running from their tents.

"What's happening, Soldier?" asked a sergeant running towards the sentry.

"Over there, sir," pointed the sentry. "Silas is dead, sir, someone cut his head from his body."

The sergeant looked where the sentry was pointing; something big moved within the fog. "There," pointed the sergeant. An ungodly guttural growl came from within the thick fog.

Twelve huge horned beasts charged into the camp, swinging crude wooden clubs. The sergeant's head exploded in a shower of crimson as the wooden club smashed into it, his body crumpled to the floor. Soldiers ran forward to hack and slash at the creatures, their sabres barely penetrating the thick skin.

One of the creatures let out a terrible roar and surged forward, swinging its club in murderous arcs, killing all in its path. More soldiers advanced on the beasts, dying as they came in range of the swinging clubs. Ten soldiers ran for their mounts and took up lances. Quickly, they heeled their panic-stricken horses into a charge. One of the soldiers drove his lance into the chest of the closest creature. The lance snapped, jutting out of the creature's chest. It screamed out in pain and brought its club down on the soldier, killing him and his mount before the creature fell to the floor.

Four more riders were knocked from the saddle; their bodies smashed as the terrible clubs cloved into them, killing rider and horse. Another of the creatures screamed out as two soldiers drove their lances deep into its back.

"Get to the horses," shouted one man, trying to organise the soldiers. "You, men, grab torches," the soldier continued. "Line up, defensive formation. Keep them under pressure."

Fifty soldiers ran forward with flaming torches in their hands, waving them at the creatures while other soldiers ran for their scattered mounts.

More than a hundred of the king's guard had been killed by the small group of ogres for only the loss of two of their number. Now the soldiers were holding the ogres back with fire and sword. The soldiers that had run for their mounts were struggling to keep the horses calm. The creatures had un-nerved the horses; most had scattered, only the best trained of the horses had not leapt the fence and bolted.

One ogre stepped forward, swinging his club with terrible speed and catching the soldiers off guard. With one swing, ten soldiers had been downed, creating a gap in the line of torches. The rest of the ogres surged forward, smashing soldiers from their feet. The cries from the wounded and dying were haunting and filled the thick fog with an eerie sound. The rest of the soldiers panicked and broke formation, running to escape the terrible clubs of the ogres. Chaos had erupted within the camp as soldiers fled out of harm's way. The ogres gave chase, smashing their clubs into the fleeing soldiers.

One soldier tripped over the body of a fallen comrade. Turning, he saw the huge ogre looming over him, its arms had thick black hair covering its brown skin, two huge tusk-like teeth jutted from its bottom jaw and smooth black ram-like horns curled down from the sides of its temples. The ogre let out a terrible roar and brought its club up above its head, ready to strike at the man on the floor. A white shafted arrow thudded into the ogre's eye. The club slipped from its hand and it fell backwards without a sound.

The sound of a war horn cut through the thick fog as twenty elven archers loosed arrow after arrow into the ogres, then the sound of hooves striking the ground could be heard as King Tyrin came charging from out of the fog. The huge form of Shadow charged directly at the ogres, his speed unfaltering. One ogre lunged for the grey stallion, its arm outstretched. Tyrin brought his sword up which passed through flesh muscle and bone to sever the ogre's arm in one sweep. The ogre fell back, screaming in pain as Shadow reared up on his hind legs, striking the ogre in the face with his iron-shod hooves. The elven warriors loosed shaft upon shaft at the ogres with bewildering speed. The ogres fell to the elven archers, their bodies littered with arrows. Tyrin wheeled Shadow round, looking at the devastation to the camp.

"Where is Sargent Cabrus?" asked Tyrin.

"Dead, Your Majesty," said a dark-haired soldier. "He was one of the first to fall, Your Majesty."

Tyrin looked at the fear on the soldier's face. "What's your name, Soldier?" asked Tyrin.

"Coteus, Your Majesty," replied the soldier.

"Well, Coteus, I want a count of all the men who are injured and a count of the dead."

"Yes, Your Majesty," replied Coteus. "At once."

General Kaylin rode into the camp accompanied by King Alinar. Anger showed on his face as he reined in his chestnut mare. "That was a reckless charge," he admonished Tyrin. "You could have been killed."

"Ah, my friend, you worry too much," Tyrin told him with a smile on his face, trying to lighten the general's mood.

"May I see your sword, Your Majesty?" asked Alinar, dismounting from the white horse he rode.

Tyrin gave the elf king a questioning look, then reversing the sword, he passed it to Alinar hilt-first. Alinar looked closely at the blade and noticed the black stains in the metal. "I have never seen a blade cut so deeply and cleanly through an ogre's flesh. The flesh of these creatures are notoriously tough, and it would take great strength and a blade as sharp as a shaving razor to sever an arm as you did."

"The sword has been stained with the blood of Sagoth ever since I stabbed it through his back, it will not wipe clean."

"May I?" asked Alinar, pointing to the body of the ogre.

Tyrin nodded his head. Alinar stepped towards the body of the ogre. "It is said that ogre horn is stronger than steel and will shatter swords if one is struck against it." Alinar held the sword out above the ogre's head and let the blade drop.

"No," Tyrin called out as the blade dropped towards one of the horns of the ogre. The blade passed through the horn, severing it cleanly. Tyrin looked at Alinar and then at Kaylin, the shock on his face was apparent. "How?" he asked.

"It must be the blood of Sagoth; your blade is special, Your Majesty. Guard it well for I have never seen a blade like this in all my years."

"With your permission, Your Majesty," said Kaylin. "I will take charge of the camp and report the losses."

Tyrin nodded his agreement as the general made his way into the camp. Alinar reversed the sword and handed it back to Tyrin.

"I think we need the council of Elazar," said Tyrin, sheathing his sword.

Chapter Twenty-Three

The devastation caused by the ogres was colossal, out of the four hundred and ninety soldiers that had remained in the camp, two hundred and sixty-five had been killed. Thirty-seven were seriously injured and would not survive the journey back to Carthage. Alinar had agreed that the elves would care for the wounded until they were well enough to attempt the journey home and that the magic of forest would aid with their recovery. It was a few days after the fight with the ogres that Tyrin led the remainder of his soldiers home. The mood on the journey was a sombre one as they rode.

Shamari had been working tirelessly to open the gateway between the two nations; she would wake just before dawn and head out, casting the spells needed into the great stone gate. Each day, Derrel would bring her food before he headed out with the dwarves' scouting parties. He was certain his younger brother was still alive, the blackened and burnt bodies at the dock had been counted. All were accounted for except one.

"He's alive," Derrel had told Shamari. "I know it, Tal is more slippery than an eel."

"If he is still alive, the drows will have taken him," she had replied. "But please, my love, it has been near on eight months since the attack at the docks. I do not want to crush your hopes but in all likeliness the drows may have killed him."

Derrel felt his anger rising but knew that Shamari spoke the truth. "I will search for him until the gate is ready and once you open it, I will take a full detachment of soldiers and hunt these drows down."

Now her pregnancy was in the final stages which drained her even more. Shamari knew that once she cast the last spell and the gate opened that Derrel would stop at nothing to find his brother or avenge him. She finished casting the spell she was working on and released it towards the stone pillars. Both pillars started to vibrate, resonating with power stored within them. Shamari took a deep breath and stepped back; this was it! One more spell and the gate would open.

Pain flared within her stomach, causing her to cry out in pain. Shamari placed her hand on her swollen belly and the pain flared again.

"Not now, little one, please." The babe insider kicked as if responding. Taking a deep breath, she headed towards the door of the warehouse. The pain came again, causing her to double over. With one hand on the door, she managed to pull it open. The three moons had already risen, casting their blue, silver and pink light. Still clutching her stomach, Shamari stumbled off to her home in search of Derrel.

Stepping from the bath, Derrel rubbed himself dry with the soft white cotton towel. His skin had a permanent bronze colour to it from his endless days in the sun searching for his brother. He knew Shamari would be home soon and that she would tell him of the progress of the gateway. Derrel heard the door open then he heard the panic in the voice of the dwarf servant. Quickly, he dressed and made his way through the home he shared with Shamari. He found her just inside the doorway, doubled over and clutching at her stomach. The young dwarf woman who looked after the house was trying to help Shamari to a seat.

"Please, mistress, you must sit, the baby is coming," said the young dwarf woman. "I will find Master Derrel then I will go for the healer."

"No need," said Derrel as he made his way towards the two women. "Where dose the healer live? I will be faster than you."

"She lives two streets over from where Chief Detas lives. Get to the chief's lodge and go to the north, there you will find the home of the healer. She is called Jaboulda, her home has a green painted door."

Derrel knelt down and took Shamari by the hand and kissed it. Her breathing was heavy as she panted, trying to control the contractions. "Hold on, my love, I will be back soon with the healer." Shamari smiled and nodded. Derrel turned to the young dwarf woman. "Stay with her," he said sternly then he turned and left.

It took thirty minutes for Derrel to reach the home of the healer and bring her back to help Shamari. The healer woman had ordered Derrel from the bedroom; he now paced back and forth as the woman he loved screamed out in pain. He could hear the healer talking to Shamari, telling her to control her breathing. It seemed like an eternity to Derrel, then it came the wail of a new born babe. Slowly, the door opened, and the healer came to stand before Derrel. "You can come in now, young master, and meet your son," she told him, smiling.

Shamari lay on the bed the babe at her breast, her dark hair was sweat-drenched. She smiled as Derrel approached.

"Are you OK?" asked Derrel in a hushed voice.

"I am well, my love," Shamari answered. "Would you like to hold your son?"

Derrel looked at the suckling babe. "I will wait until he has had his fill," he replied.

"Would you like to name him?" Shamari asked.

"Atuirus," said Derrel. "It was my grandfather's name."

Shamari smiled. "Atuirus, that is a good name. I have more good news, my love. The gateway needs only one more spell to activate it."

Derrel's eyes went wide with excitement. "I will rest for a couple of days, then I will contact Elazar for him to be ready at the gate in Carthage."

Derrel lent forward and kissed her brow, the babe moved his head away from Shamari's breast and Derrel took him from his mother. "Sleep, my love, I will take care of our son." She smiled at him and closed her eyes.

Elazar had read the message from King Alinar, which had informed him of the ogres venturing out of the southern wastelands, but what intrigued Elazar the most was the news regarding Tyrin's sword, and how it had passed through the ogre horn unblemished, and how the blood of Sagoth had stained the blade, becoming part of the very sword itself.

The master mage admired Tyrin. He was a good king for someone so young, but Elazar could not forget Tyrin's unwillingness in stopping the curse of Sagoth. It had been so simple; all he had to do was to never sire any children. Over a year had now passed since the demon had fallen and the departure of Kadius. He and Davira had not yet found anyone to replace his former student to the position of master mage. Elazar sighed at the memory of his old friend and felt the pang of guilt at his loss.

"Stop this melancholy," he told himself; soon it would be time for him and Davira to journey to Carthage. Shamari had sent word to her sister mage that only one more spell was needed to activate the gate in Rainoa.

A knock came from the door to Elazar's private rooms. "Enter," he said. The door opened, Lady Davira stepped in through the door and bowed in a greeting.

"Are you ready?" she asked. "It is now noon, so it will be quite late in Rainoa, and Shamari has been working tirelessly to complete the gate. She has also told me that she has a surprise to share with us once we see each other."

"Interesting," said Elazar, smiling. "We could use some good news. Have you any idea what she has to tell us?"

"No," said Davira, smiling, "but she has been gone far too long now and my heart aches to see her once more."

Elazar nodded his agreement; the two mages closed their eyes and spoke the words of power and disappeared.

The sun was approaching its apex high in the late summer sky when the two master mages appeared just outside the palace ground, startling the guards on duty at the main gate. The four guards soon regained their composure.

A blond-haired guard stepped forward and bowed. "I will send word to the palace that you have arrived, my lord and lady." Turning to one of the other soldiers, he ordered him to run on and inform the king that the two mages had arrived.

"Why did we not just teleport directly into the throne room?" Davira asked. "Tyrin is expecting us, and it would be far simpler."

"It would," replied Elazar. "But the throne room will be busy, and I do not fancy teleporting directly on top of someone; it gets messy when that happens."

The two mages thanked the soldiers who stood guard for admitting them to the city and walked through the gate. As the two blue-robed mages walked the streets, the citizens of Carthage had mixed reactions to them; some would stop and stare, while others would smile and ask for a blessing, and others would run in the opposite direction. At last, the palace came into view and a dark-haired herald dressed in purple leggings and tunic with black leather shoes ran forward to meet them. The shoes had an overly large silver buckle on the front which Davira thought looked ridiculous.

"Greetings, good masters," said the herald in an over-exaggerated voice. Every time he could, he over pronounced his R's, rolling his tongue around in his mouth. "King Tyrin has asked me to convey his most gracious welcome to you both; he bids that you accompany me to the throne room where both their majesties eagerly await you."

Elazar inclined his head slightly. "Then lead on, my good fellow," he told the herald.

The herald bowed once more and turned. "This way, please."

King Tyrin sat on his golden throne, dressed in a white shirt with a dark blue velvet tunic and dark blue leggings with calf-length black boots. To his left sat Queen Emelia, looking as radiant as ever. She wore a simple light blue dress trimmed with white lace, her honey-blonde hair had been pulled to one side and was held in place by a golden circlet. To the king's right stood General Kaylin. Elazar thought the old general had aged quite considerably since last he had seen him. To the queen's left, holding the young prince, stood a young maid. The young prince fidgeted in her arms. What Elazar took to be Tyrin's council members stood either side of the throne room.

As the two mages walked closer to the dais where the royal family sat, Tyrin came to his feet and a hush fell over the gathered people in the room.

"Welcome," said Tyrin, his voice ringing with authority,

"you do us a great honour by being here today to mark this wondrous occasion." The council members started to nod their heads in approval. Tyrin continued with his speech, "Today will see a new era of trade between the two nations of Sharr and Rainoa. We both have people on the other side of the world that our hearts yearn to see, and now thanks to the masters and magic users of High Castle, there will be no need for the long voyage." All in attendance within the throne room started to applaud.

Elazar raised his hand and a silence fell over the attending people. "Your Majesty is most generous in his praise, and his words are true; this is indeed a wondrous day, so I would ask His Majesty that we delay this no further and let us all make haste to the gateway."

"So be it," said Tyrin, "let us be away at once."

Chapter Twenty-Four

The stone gate stood to the very rear of the palace grounds, all the three pillars had been sculpted from stone of the Grey Mountains of the dwarfs. The stone had been made a smooth as glass and golden runes had been set into the pillars that ran to the base and continued into the stone circle the pillars were stood upon. The gold seemed to shimmer with light that swirled up and down the pillars. To one side stood a small ornate wooden table and upon it sat a bowl of water.

"Everything is as you asked for," Tyrin told the two mages.

Davira stepped forward towards the table and looked at Elazar. The master mage nodded his head. Davira started to gesture her hands over the bowl and quietly started the incantation of the spell. The water in the bowl started to shimmer and the image of a young beautiful dark-haired woman appeared.

"Greetings, my sister," said Davira, smiling warmly at the image.

"Greetings," said Shamari, smiling back. "It is good to see you."

"Is all in readiness?" Davira asked.

"It is, my sister."

Elazar stepped forward so Shamari could see him. "I will start the union spell that will align the two gates. You will know at what point to activate the gate."

Shamari nodded her understanding, her image faded from the bowl. Elazar stepped back and began to chant. The stone pillars seemed to vibrate, and the air around them seemed to crackle with energy. In the centre of the gate, a small white orb formed and started to grow its light, expanding outwards. The orb continued to grow until it touched the sides of the stone pillars, then the colour changed into a rainbow of colours that swirled around within the confines of the stone.

Derrel stood at Shamari's side, holding his infant son. He could feel the change in the air, energy seemed to be resonating from the white stone. Shamari stood with hands outstretched, chanting in a language that Derrel did not understand. He watched as a small white orb started to form in the centre of the pillars, its light becoming brighter and spreading to the four corners of the pillars. The light stopped with in the confines of the pillars, it shifted and changed in an array of colours.

Elazar could feel the pull from the other gate as the two of them aligned. Sweat had started to bead on his brow as he controlled the magic contained within the gateways. Tyrin stood with his queen and General Kaylin. As the colours shifted, Tyrin took a step backwards, he took a hold of Emelia's arm and gently pulled her back a few paces. Light started to dance from Elazar's hands and was pulled towards the gate to join in the swirling mass of colours.

"By Ristus," said Tyrin, his eyes growing wide.

Shamari could now hear the voice of Elazar echoing through the gate. The time to release the spell was now. Shamari released the magic from her body and fell to her knees. Derrel rushed forward and helped her to stand.

"I am fine, my love," she told him.

Derrel brushed her dark hair away from her face. Shamari looked tired, the birth of their son and the opening of the gateway had taken a lot out of her.

Elazar felt the magic released from Shamari and released his own spell. A great whoosh of air came from the gateway, blowing Elazar's blue robes and causing the mage to take a step backwards. Elazar heard the rasp of a sword being drawn from its scabbard. He turned to see General Kaylin with his sword drawn. Kaylin had positioned himself in front of his king and queen.

"It is quite all right, General," Elazar told him. "It is safe."

"Look," said Emelia, pointing towards the gate. The array of lights had formed into a silver mist that swirled and danced within the gate. A dark shadow could be seen within the mist, like a person walking through a fog bank. The shadow became more solid. From the mist stepped Derrel. He was dressed strangely; he wore a black leather kilt studded with silver and a strange-looking tunic that had no sleeves, leaving his arms bare. His skin had a healthy bronze glow to it and his hair had been close cropped to his head. Behind him came a tall dark-haired woman dressed in the blue robes of the mages of High Castle, and in her arms she carried a new-born babe.

"Derrel," shouted Kaylin, sheathing his sword and running forward to embrace his son. Derrel stepped forward and hugged his father. The joy on the old general's face was apparent; he did not try to hide his emotions at the joy of his eldest son's return. A cough from behind the two men broke the embrace.

"Your Majesty, I apologise," said Derrel, bowing. "Please excuse me."

"No need, Sergeant," replied Tyrin. "Your return has been too long in waiting; your father has been too long without you."

"Thank you, Your Majesty," said Derrel. "May I present to you Lady Shamari of High Castle" – he gestured to the woman behind him – "also my wife. And may I present our son,

Atuirus?"

There was a sharp intake of breath form all in attendance; it was Davira who spoke first to break the silence. "I take it that this is the news you wished to share with us," she said, smiling and stepping forward to embrace Shamari.

"Indeed, it is," Shamari told her.

"Excuse me, my lady," said General Kaylin, stepping forward and gesturing to the infant sleeping in her arms. "May I?" he asked.

"Of course," she replied, offering the babe to him. Kaylin took the sleeping babe and walked off a little ways.

Tyrin and Elazar watched as the old general took the babe and excused himself. Derrel bowed to the king. "Your Majesty, I am ready to brief you in full of what has transpired in Rainoa, it will take quite some time to report everything that has happened. When I am finished, it should be a reasonable time in Rainoa should His Highness wish to journey there and meet Chief Detas of the dwarves."

Tyrin looked at the shimmering gate with some scepticism. "That would be interesting," said Tyrin. "I think you and I should go to my private apartments for the briefing."

"As His Majesty commands," said Derrel.

Tyrin looked at his wife. "My love, would you ask Kaylin to join us after he has finished introducing himself to his grandson?"

Emelia smiled and nodded. "Would you care to join us after you have spoken with Lady Shamari?" he asked Elazar. The master mage nodded his head.

In the king's apartments, Tyrin handed a goblet of wine to Derrel. "Tell me what happened with the ships."

Derrel sipped at the wine and sighed, then he relayed the story of how the ships had docked at the beach and of the arrival of the dwarves, and of his fight with the dwarf chief's son and of the arrival of Lady Shamari also his journey to the dwarf city. Finally, he told Tyrin of the attack on the ships and the slaughter of the crews and the soldiers by the drows.

Tyrin listen without interrupting the sergeant. When Derrel had finished his report, Tyrin asked of the gift he had sent for the dwarf chief. Derrel explained of how he intended to give the war hammer as a parting gift to the chief. Tyrin nodded his understanding.

"Your Majesty, if I may ask, why is the golden hammer so important? I have seen the abundance of gold in Rainoa, the dwarves use it as we use steel or tin. Gold has little value to them."

"Your father and I made a decision that could affect the fate of our world; it was a decision that we did not take lightly, but I will discuss that after Elazar and the other mages return to High Castle."

"But Your Majesty, Lady Shamari is my wife and the mother of my son."

"And you are a sergeant in the king's army. You swore an oath to defend the crown and the kingdom. your father stood by my father's side and their fathers before them and their fathers before them; our families have been linked for generations. Will you be the first to break that oath?"

Derrel's face flushed red with anger, and Tyrin saw his sword hand twitch. "I am a king's soldier, I swore to protect you and this kingdom. My oath is my bond and should any man question that oath, I would put my sword through their heart." Derrel's eyes were cold as he looked at the king.

"Good," said Tyrin. "That is the reaction I wanted from you, now draw your sword."

Derrel looked questionably at his king. What was the man thinking, was he about to be challenged? He knew Tyrin was a good swordsman, but he also knew that the king could not beat him in single combat. Derrel placed his hand on the hilt of his sword and pulled it from its scabbard.

"Do you swear on your sword that what you are told in this room will remain with you until the day you die, or your king commands you to reveal the information?"

"I do, Your Majesty, now and always," Derrel replied, dropping to one knee without hesitation.

The door to the king's private apartments opened and in stepped General Kaylin. he looked at his son and king. "Have I missed something?" asked Kaylin.

Quickly, Tyrin told Derrel of how he and his father had hidden the gem in the golden hammer and of their decision to send it where they hoped no one would ever find it.

"If I had but known, Your Majesty, I would not have waited in the giving of the gift," Derrel told his king.

"The fault lies with me, Derrel, not you. I swore to protect the dam gem and my decision was a poor one."

"Your Majesty, with your permission, I will take a full regiment of soldiers and track down the hammer, but I have been searching these past nine months and I have not seen a single drow. As you know, they are responsible for the death of our men and the disappearance of my brother."

"Is there a chance Tal could still be alive?" asked Kaylin. Tyrin could hear the hope in his friend's voice.

"The dwarves tell me not, Father; they say that the drows kill all for they hate all but their own. I spent every waking minute I could searching and found nothing."

A knock came at the door. "Enter," said Tyrin. The door

opened and a servant popped his head round.

"Master Elazar and the other mages are here to see you."

"Please show them in," answered Tyrin. Turning to Kaylin and Derrel, he said, "We will talk more on this later."

The three master mages of High Castle entered the king's apartments. "Has the sergeant finished his report?" asked Elazar.

"He has," said Tyrin. "We were just discussing the best course of action to take with regards to the drows. The sergeant here will take a regiment of soldiers and track them down."

"Shamari tells me that the dwarves are more than a match for the drows. Is there a need to send soldiers to a foreign land?" asked Elazar.

It was Derrel that answered. "With all respect, sir, my brother is still not accounted for and I promised my father I would find him."

"Then it looks like I will be needed here," said Shamari, stepping close to her husband and linking her arm through his. "With your permission, Your Majesty, I will remain here in Carthage." Tyrin nodded his agreement.

"You can stay at my estate," said Kaylin. "My servants will attend to you and my grandson. By the way, mightn't I ask who has him at the moment?"

Shamari smiled. "He is with the queen and the young prince; it would seem that the prince has taken a great interest in his new friend."

"Your Majesty," said Derrel. "I think we should make preparations to meet Chief Detas; the dwarves are not known for their patience."

"The sergeant is right," said Tyrin.

The king called the servant back and issued his orders for the crates of steel to be brought from the royal smithies, then he looked at Kaylin. "General, please assemble the soldiers that will accompany Derrel on his mission back to Rainoa. They can leave after I have returned, I don't want to send soldiers through the gate without the chief's permission."

Kaylin bowed. "At once, Your Majesty. My lady," he said to Shamari, "would you please accompany me? I will show you to my home so you and your son can settle in."

Shamari smiled. "Thank you, General."

"Please call me Kaylin," he replied. "We are family now."

Shamari kissed Derrel on the cheek. "Be careful, my love," she told him, "you know how dangerous the jungle can be. Don't get careless." She made to leave, then stopped. "One last thing before I go." She looked at Tyrin. "Please do not be alarmed, Your Majesty," she told him, gesturing with her hands.

Tyrin raised an eyebrow as smoke came from the mage's hands and drifted towards him; it seemed to encircle his head then disappear. "That will help when you meet the chief," she told him. "It will also stop Derrel having to translate everything the chief says."

Chapter Twenty-Five

Tyrin stood in front of the magical gateway. He now wore his soft black leather leggings, black calf-length boots with a black leather jerkin, and his silver breast plate had been polished to a high shine. The four royal guards stood just behind, dressed identical to the king. Derrel approached, still dressed in his leather kilt and vest. His arming sword strapped to his back. Tyrin looked at the young sergeant.

"Do all the dwarves dress as you are dressed?"

"Yes, Your Majesty," replied Derrel, smiling. "It's the heat. Dressed as you are, My King, you will be extremely warm."

"Does it ever get cold there?" asked Tyrin.

"Only when it rains," Derrel told him. "The rain is so heavy that you cannot see more than ten paces in front of you."

Tyrin turned to his wife who stood with his son in her arms and smiled. "Please be careful," she mouthed to him. Tyrin nodded then turned back to Derrel. "After you, sergeant," he said, gesturing to the gate. Derrel stepped forward and vanished into the swirling mist, followed by Tyrin and the four soldiers.

Shamari had taken to motherhood whole-heartedly; she sat in the horse-drawn carriage with her fellow mage Davira as they made their way to General Kaylin's estate. The old general rode steadily in front on his chestnut mare, talking to Elazar who rode a young palomino stallion. The master mage kept the young horse at a tight rein. "He seems very spirited," said Elazar.

"Indeed," laughed Kaylin, trying his best to hide the smile

on his face.

"I think I will stick to walking and teleporting," Elazar told him.

"But you look so natural sat on horseback," shouted Davira from the window of the carriage.

Elazar did his best to turn in the saddle, he caught a quick glimpse of Davira's head as she disappeared back inside the carriage, then he heard the laughter of the two women.

Kaylin's home came into view. The farming estate consisted of a large central white building with the outer buildings built around it in a u shape. To the right stood the stables for the horses which led out onto a large paddock, Elazar noticed a huge grey stallion stood cropping the grass. "The king's horse," Kaylin told the mage. "I have been putting him to stud, I have nine mares due to give birth in a few months."

"I never really understood the need for horses," Elazar said, still struggling with the spirited stallion.

"I have never known a horse like the king's mount. He is a little peculiar, and I must add probably the most intelligent horse I've ever known. It is my intention to breed a more intelligent war mount for the king's army."

The carriage pulled up in front of the main building and an elderly gentleman came out to greet them. He was dressed in a dark grey doublet and leggings. He bowed as Kaylin stepped from the saddle. "General, the rooms have been prepared as you requested."

"Thank you, Timkins, please let me introduce you to Lady Shamari and my grandson, Atuirus." Timkins bowed. "And this is Lady Davira and Master Elazar from High Castle.

"Please follow me and I will show you to your rooms," said Timkins, bowing again.

"That's all right," Elazar replied. "Lady Davira and I will be returning to High Castle, we still have much to do."

"As you wish, my lord." Timkins held out a hand to Shamari. "This way, my lady, I'm sure that the young master will be eager to sleep after the journey from the palace."

"One moment, please," said Shamari. Turning to Elazar, she handed the babe to Kaylin, who was more than happy to take him. "Once I'm settled, I will come to High Castle and report on how things are going with the dwarves of Rainoa." Elazar nodded his head.

Davira stepped in and embraced Shamari. "Farewell, sister, please don't stay away too long. We have to find a new master now that Kadius has left us."

"I will see you soon." Davira stepped back from Shamari and stood with Elazar. The two mages closed their eyes and spoke the words of power and vanished from sight.

"My lady," said Timkins, gesturing towards the house.

An eerie coldness swept over Tyrin as he stepped into the swirling mist. All sound seemed to disappear as if he were under water, then he felt a strange pulling at his body as if invisible hands had taken hold of him and were pulling him forward. The grey silver mist seemed to shimmer and grow brighter then disappear. Tyrin found himself stood in what looked like a warehouse of some sort. The four soldiers stepped from the gateway, blinking in wonderment.

"Your Majesty, welcome to Rainoa." Tyrin blinked. "Your Majesty, are you OK?" Tyrin looked around and then focused on Derrel. "Your Majesty, are you OK?"

"Yes, thank you, Sergeant," Tyrin replied. "That was the strangest feeling."

The doors to the warehouse opened, Tyrin found himself looking at seven dark-skinned dwarfs, all wearing the same style of clothing as Derrel. The dwarves looked at the six newcomers with suspicion, then one of them recognised Derrel.

"Derrel, you're back," said one of the dwarves, pushing his way to the front. "Darumi told us you were going back to the other side of the world, but you have only been gone half a day."

"I know, my friend, that is the power of the gate that Shamari built. I would like to present His Majesty King Tyrin Degarre of Sharr."

The dwarf stepped forward and thrust out his hand. "My name is Gronim, it is good to meet Derrel's king."

Tyrin stepped forward and took Gronim's hand in a warrior's grip. "Well met, Gronim. Will you and your men take us to your chief?"

"My men will remain here to watch the gate. I will take you to Chief Detas. Come, I have mounts outside."

Derrel smiled as they made to leave the warehouse.

If Tyrin was shocked at the sight of the war birds, he did not let it show. He calmly mounted the bird he was offered and rode it as if he had ridden one all his life.

Gronim took the short journey from the warehouse to the chief's lodge at a steady pace. Derrel had felt the awesome power and speed of the birds and wondered if Tyrin could handle them at full speed. The only time Tyrin showed any kind of shock was when he saw the abundance of gold that had been used in the construction of the homes and buildings of the dwarves.

The six birds trotted through the streets, squawking at the town's people that got in their way. The dwarves would nimbly dodge out of the bird's path and then carry on with whatever they were doing. This brought back memories for Derrel of the day he and the king had rode back into Carthage with the other soldiers at speed. The galloping horses had charged through the markets, the soldiers shouting out warnings as they approached, then the fat little trader Aaron Jones had thrown an orange out of anger, striking Tyrin on the back.

Derrel had dragged on the reins of his mount and ordered the fruit trader to report to him later that day. That evening, the fruit trader had come to the palace with his daughter in tow. Derrel had to admit that Emelia had been the most stunningly beautiful woman he had seen and when Tyrin had turned up and defused the situation, Derrel had felt a pang of jealously.

Then Tyrin had asked the woman to join him for dinner, and now Emelia was his queen. The chief's lodge came into view. Detas was stood outside, talking to the servants that tendered to the grounds of his estate when he noticed the seven war birds approaching. a huge smile set on the chief's face as he saw Derrel.

"My friend, back so soon. I would not have thought to see you back this quick," bellowed Detas.

Derrel reined in his mount along with the other riders and slid from the bird's back. He extended his hand to the chief, but it was brushed to one side as Detas stepped in and embraced the young sergeant. Derrel felt the breath squeezed from his lungs as the chief's powerful arms went round him.

"It is good to see you again," said Derrel, trying to catch his breath. Detas released his grip and turned to the newcomers. "Chief Detas, may I present to you King Tyrin Degarre of Sharr."

Detas looked at the man in front of him and smiled. "Good to meet you, my boy." Detas stepped in and hugged Tyrin as if they were old friends reuniting. "So you're the man who sent me all that lovely steel."

"Chief Detas," said Tyrin, bowing his head. "Our meeting has been long overdue."

"Yes," Detas replied. "It was a damn shame about your men and your ships. Oh and the lost gold, of course. My men were able to retrieve most of the gold that sunk when the drows torched your ships, it's waiting near the warehouse for you."

"You are too kind, and I have another shipment of steel waiting to come through."

"Excellent. Come, come, let us eat and drink to our new friendship and discuss terms," Detas told them. "And let's see if we can find something more comfortable for you to wear. You look positively roasting in those funny clothes you wear." Detas Turned and walked off without waiting to see if he was being followed.

Tyrin looked at Derrel and raised an eyebrow. "You will get used to the lack of formality, my king," Derrel told him. "The only one with any title is Detas as chief. The responsibility of his kingdom falls on his shoulders, he makes all the decisions."

"Interesting," replied Tyrin, as they followed the dwarf chief. "And those birds we rode in on, I could feel the power in them. I would like to push one to its limit and test its speed." Tyrin glanced over his shoulder and watched as servants came and led the birds away.

The negotiations between Tyrin and Detas lasted for quite some time, but finally the two leaders agreed on their terms. Detas had been more than happy for the steel and gold to be exchanged for equal amounts, but it took more persuasion for Detas to let a full regiment of Tyrin's soldiers come through the gate and have a permeant barracks on Rainoa. It was only when Tyrin had pointed out that these men would be at the disposal of the dwarf chief and that their sole purpose would be to track down the drows.

Tyrin had offered in exchange for the barracks on Rainoa that Detas would be granted lands on the planes of Varith where he would be free to breed and raise his war birds and the livestock to feed them. This seemed to please the dwarf chief. The two leaders sealed the treaty with a drink and a shake of hands.

"I will send the steel as soon as I'm back through the gate."

"And I will have the gold brought to accompany you back. Let this be the beginning of a great friendship between our two kingdoms."

Detas then looked at Derrel. "I have a small gift for you too, my young friend." The chief signalled to one of the young women who stood next to the door. She bowed and left the room. "That sword you carry is a fine weapon and I remember you telling me that you had armed your brother with your sabre on the day of the attack, and that sabre will now be in the hands of the drows."

The door to the room opened and the young dwarf woman entered carrying a wooden box. She laid the box on the table in front of Derrel and smiled.

Derrel flipped open the lid of the box to reveal two scabbarded swords. The scabbards were wrapped in a soft white leather and had intricate golden decorations that ran down the full length of the scabbard. The hand guards swept around and were shaped like the heads of the war birds. These shone as bright as silver. The handles were made from bone and were inlayed with silver thread and topped with a silver disc pommel, baring two crossed swords encircled within a crown.

Derrel removed one from the box and drew it from its scabbard. The blade was three feet in length. Just below the guard, the blade was two inches wide and three inches long with no edge, then the blade flared out to three inches. Its edges razor-sharp and ending in a rounded point. The blade had a fuller in the centre that ran its full length. Derrel hefted the sword, it was perfectly balanced.

"You will find no finer blade, my boy," Detas told him with a huge smile on his face. "Dwarven smiths are the finest there are."

Derrel could hear the pride in the chief's voice. "You honour me, my lord chief," said Derrel, returning the sword to its scabbard. He then removed his arming sword from his back and settled the twin blades in place.

"That is a fine gift," said Tyrin. "I'm sure that the sergeant will put them to good use in the days to come."

Chapter Twenty-Six

Kaylin had retired to his estates, stepping down as the king's general. He now devoted his time to the breading of horses using Shadow as the stud, and any spare time he had was spent with his grandson. Lady Shamari had settled into her new life as a mother, leaving her son with his overprotective grandfather while she returned to High Castle to perform her duties. The old general doted over the boy.

With his father stepping down, Derrel had been promoted to captain and to the position of king's champion. The young captain would return to his father's estates as often as possible, spending time with his wife and son, but as always, he would return to Rainoa in search of his missing brother. Two years had passed and still the shipments of gold and silver continued in trade for steel. The king's treasury was now overflowing, much to the jealousy of the surrounding dukes and barons.

The first foals from Shadow were now maturing and ready to be broken in, Kaylin had noticed that these young horses seemed to have some of their sire's traits and showed to be a more intelligent bread.

Tyrin had come to his old friend's home one autumn day, requesting that Kaylin join him on a trip to the Planes of Varith to check on the dwarves settlement and the breading of the war birds. Kaylin had taken an instant dislike to the birds.

"Horses are more reliable and easier to train. They may not be as fast, but I would wager a horse could outlast one of those accursed beasts," Kaylin had said.

The trip had taken them two weeks and the birds seemed to be flourishing on the planes. On the night of his return, Kaylin found Shamari sat in the main living quarters of the house with her two-year-old son fast asleep on her lap. She was reading an old leather-bound book from the light of the fire burning away in the hearth. Derrel's old arming sword hung on the wall above the fire place. The mage smiled as Kaylin entered the room.

"Would you like me to take him and put him to bed?" Kaylin asked.

"Yes, please," replied Shamari. "Derrel was here this morning and I think that Atuirus got over excited. He was quite upset when his father had to leave again." Gently, Shamari lifted the sleeping toddler and passed him to Kaylin.

The child moaned in his sleep as Kaylin took him. The old man smiled as the boy nuzzled his head against his chest.

"*Shhhh*, little one." Kaylin gently rocked the boy in his arms as he left the room to put the boy to his bed. He returned to the room where Shamari still sat reading her book and took a seat opposite her.

She paused in her reading. "How goes it with the dwarves? Have they gotten used to the change in temperature?"

"They seem to be copping rather well. It would seem that the dwarves from Rainoa are as hardy a people as the dwarves from Grey Mountain, though I must say I do not care for those damn birds they ride."

Shamari gave him a broad smile. "They do take some getting used to."

Timkins came into the room bearing a silver tray with a jug of wine and two cups. He poured one each for Kaylin and Shamari and set the jug down. "Will there be anything else, my lord?" Timkins asked.

"No, thank you," Kaylin told him.

"Then with your permission, my lord, I will retire for the night."

Kaylin nodded his head, "I have seen you read books for the past couple of years, my dear; have you not found what it is that you are looking for?"

Shamari lowered the book. "It is the curse of Sagoth that I am trying to figure out, the other masters found a reference on an ancient scroll that spoke of an innocent. We have had all the students searching the entire library."

"Has anything else been found?"

Shamari shook her head. "We have found references on prophecies that have come to pass and some yet to come, and some that are complete ravings of mad men and women."

A dull thud came from the kitchen followed by the clanging of something metal dropping on the floor, Shamari placed the book down and made to rise.

"It's probably Timkins dropping the tray as he put it back in his stores," said Kaylin. "He has gotten a little clumsy in his old age, I'll check on him." Kaylin made to rise.

Just then, six hooded armed men, all wearing black, burst into the room. Their faces were covered, leaving only the eyes showing. Kaylin reacted; first he thrust his left hand towards the fire and grabbed hold of a burning log and hurled it at the armed men as they came forward. The six men faltered in their approach as the burning log came flying towards them. Kaylin snatched down the arming sword and placed himself between the armed men and Shamari.

"Kill the old man and the woman then find the child," said one of the men.

Shamari's eyes went wide. She raised her hand and uttered a few words. A blast of energy shot from her palm, striking the man who was trying to leave the room. The man flew through the air and slumped to the floor without another sound.

"Go to Atuirus, I can handle these," Kaylin told her.

Shamari with hands still raised slowly moved to the opposite side of the room, then ran through the open doorway. The five remaining men started to spread out, moving furniture out of their way, giving themselves room to fight. "Give up, old man, and your death will be quick," said one of the men.

Kaylin smiled. "Careful, boy, I'm old for a reason." He spat.

One of the men rushed in, slashing a short sword at Kaylin's midsection. The attack was sloppy and Kaylin easily blocked then countered, flicking his wrist and sliding the point of his sword up and through the man's neck. His attacker dropped his blade and stumbled back, his fingers trying to stop the flow of blood. Another man ran in, bringing his sabre down in an overhead strike. Kaylin blocked and countered again by slashing his sword at his attacker's midsection. This attacker was more nimble than the last and jumped back as Kaylin's blade slashed his jerkin.

A second man ran in, brandishing a wicked curved knife. Kaylin spun on his heel, the arming sword slicing through the air and through the man's arm, severing his hand at the wrist. The curved blade clattered to the floor and the man fell back, screaming and clutching at his severed wrist. The other three men spread out. Kaylin watched as three men circled him. One was armed with a sabre, one had a long hunting knife and the last had a stout wooden club. The man armed with the sabre leapt forward and Kaylin engaged him, the sound of steel clashing echoed in the room as the two swordsmen fought.

"You look tired, old man," snarled the man with the sabre. Kaylin ignored the taunt, looking the man straight in the eye. The man's gaze flicked to his left. Kaylin stepped back as the man with the club lunged forward, the swing from the club carried the attacker past Kaylin, who sliced his sword across the man's back. Kaylin felt the sword bite deep and the man screamed out in pain, his body slumped and he fell into the man with the hunting knife, knocking him to the floor.

"You are as good as they say," said the man with the sabre. "But you are old and getting slow."

"Ask your companions how slow I am," answered Kaylin, smiling. "I've killed two of them and your squealing friend there is missing his hand."

"Kill the old bastard, Tolk," screamed the man with the missing hand.

"Quiet, you fool, this old bastard is a cunning one."

"Old is something you'll never be," said Kaylin, delivering a savage attack, forcing his opponent back. The man with the sabre had some skill, Kaylin had to admit that, as the man blocked his attacks. In his youth, this man would now be dead but age now was taking its toll on the former general. Movement to his right broke his concentration as the man with the hunting knife was getting back to his feet. Pain flared in Kaylin's left shoulder as the sabre made it through his defence. Kaylin's left arm was now throbbing, he could feel the blood running down his arm. The man with the sabre was right, he was getting slower.

"Time to die," said Tolk, attacking again. Kaylin blocked and countered everything Tolk threw at him, but his strength was now starting to fail him. Kaylin feigned an attack which Tolk moved to block, opening up his defence. Quickly, Kaylin flicked his sword, slicing open a cut on Tolk's forearm. He rolled his wrist, bringing the sword down to slice through Tolk's leggings, opening a deep cut on his right thigh. Tolk's eyes went wide and Kaylin could see fear there as the would-be assassin backed away.

Tolk knew he was out-classed; he had never fought anyone with the skill the old man possessed. He had been told the job would be easy; an old man a woman and a child. Kill them all and leave no witnesses. Tolk had taken many such jobs in his life, killing men, women and children. He didn't mind so long as he was paid. It should have been so simple; kill the man and woman, then kill the sleeping child and any servants. He had taken the job and had found out that it was the legendary General Kaylin Mendez.

"I heard you were the best," one of the two men had said. Tolk had taken an instant dislike to the two men, they both had beady eyes and hooked noses, but the bag of gold they offered was large and Tolk was a greedy man.

"I am the best at what I do," snarled Tolk, "but I'll take a few extra men just to be sure. I've heard stories about the old general."

"Remember, no witnesses," the beady-eyed men had said.

Tolk's leg was starting to ache, the cut in his thigh was deep; a few inches further round and it would have cut the artery in his leg. He nodded to his companion with the hunting knife. The man ran in, knife raised, screaming at Kaylin.

We have you now, thought Tolk.

What happened next completely took Tolk by surprise; the old man dropped to one knee, avoiding the wild slash from the man with the knife. As his knee touched the floor, he reversed his sword and stabbed the knife wielder through the heart. Pulling his sword free, the old general surged to his feet, his sword arching upwards. Tolk had run in for the kill, miss-judging the old man's speed. Kaylin's sword was a blur, the blade passed through Tolk's throat as the momentum of his own attack carried him forward. Tolk's sabre slipped from his fingers and with a trembling hand he reached up, his fingers feeling the warm sticky liquid running from his severed jugular.

Kaylin rested the point of his sword on the floor. He lent heavily on the pommel, taking in deep breaths. The only sound was the whimpering from the man with the severed hand. Shamari came back into the room. "Are you OK?" she asked, looking at the blood staining the grey wool of his jerkin.

"It's just a scratch. Atuirus?" he asked.

"He's fine. I have placed a protective spell around him, he will come to no harm."

Kaylin turned his attention to the man with the missing hand, his sword came up and Kaylin placed the blade on the man's chest. "Who sent you?"

The man looked at Kaylin. His blue eyes were stern, his nostril flared as he took in deep breaths and tried to ignore the pain from his hand.

Kaylin pressed the point harder on the man's chest, the man closed his eyes and winced, "I will ask you one last time," said Kaylin, stepping forward and pulling the man's hood back. He was a middle aged man with thinning dirty blond hair, his mouth had a few blackened and broken teeth in it.

"Go to hell," snarled the man, a trickle of saliva running down his chin as he squirmed under the sword point.

"Let me see if I can persuade him," said Shamari, stepping forward, her green eyes blazing.

"Do your worst, bitch," he snarled at her.

"Oh, I intend to," she said, her voice was hard and cold. She started to gesture, her fingers in front of her and a small glowing orb appeared no bigger than a pea. With a flick of her finger, the glowing orb shot forward and disappeared into the man's skull. The man's head snapped back and his eyes went wide, the scream that came from the man's mouth was hideous and full of pain. With his good hand, he clawed at the side of his head.

"Stop, please, stop. I will tell you, I will tell you."

Shamari clicked her fingers and the glowing orb returned to her hand. She placed the orb between thumb and forefinger and crushed it. Her eyes closed and she smiled.

"Dose the name Tybost mean anything to you?" she asked Kaylin.

"The duke!" Kaylin looked shocked.

"No, not the duke. Two men, tall with dark hair."

"I know the men," Kaylin told her. "They are the sons of Kainos. He lost a duel with Derrel a few years back, Tyrin ordered there would be no blood feud, it seems that the former captain's sons still hunger for revenge."

Shamari looked back at the snivelling man, he still clutched at the stump of his arm. "What about this one?" she asked, her eyes still angry.

"He did come to kill us all, including my grandson. It's a shame he did not survive the interrogation from you."

The injured man's eyes went wide as Kaylin spoke. He tried to move but Kaylin stabbed his sword through the man's chest, piercing his heart. "Derrel and the king must be told of this, I will leave for the palace immediately."

Shamari placed her hand on his arm. "First, we must see to Timkins and remove the bodies. I do not want Atuirus seeing these men."

Kaylin nodded his agreement. The two of them made their way to the kitchen. Timkins was lying face down on the stone floor, the silver tray a few feet away from him. Kaylin turned the old man over. As he did, Timkins groaned. There was a large welt on the side of his head and the skin had split and a small trickle of blood had run down the side of his face.

Shamari looked at the wound. "I don't think the blow cracked his skull, let's get him to his quarters and into a bed. I can mix a potion that will ease the pain, but he will need to rest for a few days."

Kaylin helped the old man to his feet. "Intruders, sir," mumbled Timkins.

"It's OK," Kaylin told him. "They're gone." Timkins eyes rolled in his head and he slumped in Kaylin's arms. "Let's get you into bed, my old friend."

After an hour, Shamari and Kaylin had cleared the bodies of the six would-be assassins and had placed Timkins the estate manager in his bed. The old man had insisted his injuries were nothing and that he needed to be up to supervise the other staff on the former general's estate. Kaylin had reassured him that the estate would run fine for a few days while he rested.

The potion Shamari had given the old man had sent him to sleep, but not before he protested strongly about the bed rest. The sun had started to rise by the time they had finished removing the bodies and cleaning away the blood. Shamari had stitched the wound in Kaylin's shoulder to stop the bleeding. "It's not too deep," she told him, "but it will be sore."

Atuirus came running into the room in his white night shirt, his little bare feet padding on the floor. "Mama, I'm hungry."

Kaylin bent down and scooped the boy into his arms. He winced a little as the stiches pulled tight. "Well then, young man, let's see what we can do to fix that, shall we? What would you like to eat?"

"Porridge and honey." The child lovingly placed one tiny hand to both sides of his grandfather's face and squashed his cheeks together, then giggled. "Porridge and honey," he repeated.

"Come on then, let's see if we can find you some, shall we?" Kaylin set off to the kitchen, carrying the youngster, followed by his mother. The three of them sat at the large oak table as the youngster ate his breakfast. His little legs dangling and swinging as he ate. Kaylin had cut several slices of bread and toasted them and smeared them with honey for himself and Shamari.

"What will you tell the king?" she asked.

"I will tell him that the royal decree has been broken by the two sons of Kainos, I'm sure that Tyrin will be most annoyed by their actions."

"I remember Derrel telling me that Kainos was cousin to the Duke of Movale. Didn't you tell me that it was the duke who disapproved most to Tyrin's marriage?"

Kaylin nodded his head. "That he did, I don't know what Tyrin will do; half the nobles of the kingdom hate that he did not join his house with theirs, and the other half are jealous of the wealth that Tyrin has accumulated from the trade with the dwarves of Rainoa. This could lead to civil war.

"I will ride for the palace after I know things are taken care of here and inform the king of everything. I'll have a horse saddled and leave soon."

"Why not let me go? I can be there in the blink of an eye. I can tell the king what happened. Plus, you need to rest that shoulder. You're not getting any younger you know."

Kaylin glared at her then smiled. "I will submit to your will, my lady," he said, the good humour was apparent in his voice.

Shamari stood in the courtyard, her blue robes fluttering in the light autumn breeze. Kaylin handed her a parchment which had been sealed with his stamp. "Give this to Tyrin, it details everything that happened here last night."

Shamari nodded her head and tucked the parchment inside her robes, then raised her hands.

Atuirus came running from the house. "Mama, Mama, I want to come." He was now dressed in blue leggings and a blue tunic.

Shamari lowered her hands. "Don't you want to stay with your grandfather?"

"I want to see Obrien, he is my friend."

Kaylin smiled. "Take him, it will give me a chance to get things sorted here while you are gone."

"Come here," she told him. "Hold my hand and close your eyes." Atuirus closed his eyes so tightly that his little nose scrunched up at the effort. Raising her hand, Shamari spoke the words of power and the two of them vanished from sight.

The air seemed to shimmer where they had been stood, Kaylin heard a faint noise from one of the stables behind him. As he turned, he heard the distinctive twang of a crossbow being fired. Pain lanced through his chest. Looking down, he saw the black bolt sticking out from his body. With a trembling hand, he reached up and took hold of the bolt. He heard the crossbow discharge again and another bolt slammed into his chest. Kaylin dropped to his knees, then pitched forward. From the stable came a hooded man dressed in black leather, a crossbow in his hand. He approached the body of the former general. Kneeling down, he turned the body over and pulled his hood back. Beady eyes looked down at Kaylin's body.

"Your son killed my father, now I have killed his. Blood can only be paid for with blood." The man pulled his hood back in place, stood and ran from the estate.

Here ends Book One. Join me for Book Two, A Thief at Heart, *where we find out if the land of Sharr is thrown into civil war and where we will find out the fate of Tal Mendez.*